His voice took on a husky drawl that sent a lightning bolt of heat straight through her. "I'll do exactly what I wish, lass, and after you get over being frightened at not being the one in control, you'll realize that there's pleasure in being vulnerable. I'll pet you and touch you in ways that will make you want to scream and cry and beg for more. And when you're a breath away from losing your mind—" He paused and shook his head in slow denial. "When you're that close, sweet, I'll carry you into the bathroom and let you sizzle under a cold shower."

"What!" she squeaked. "You wouldn't really, would you?"

"Touch you like that? Of course I would."

The heat rushing through her body filled her with a kind of reckless daring she hadn't known she was capable of. Abby licked her lips and leaned so close she could feel the heat of his breath on her mouth. "I was referring to the bit about the shower."

WHAT ARE *LOVESWEPT* ROMANCES?

They are stories of true romance and touching emotion. We believe those two very important ingredients are constants in our highly sensual and very believable stories in the LOVESWEPT *line. Our goal is to give you, the reader, stories of consistently high quality that may sometimes make you laugh, sometimes make you cry, but are always fresh and creative and contain many delightful surprises within their pages.*

Most romance fans read an enormous number of books. Those they truly love, they keep. Others may be traded with friends and soon forgotten. We hope that each LOVE-SWEPT *romance will be a treasure—a "keeper." We will always try to publish*

LOVE STORIES YOU'LL NEVER FORGET
BY AUTHORS YOU'LL ALWAYS REMEMBER

The Editors

Loveswept 751

CATCH ME IF YOU CAN

VICTORIA LEIGH

BANTAM BOOKS
NEW YORK · TORONTO · LONDON · SYDNEY · AUCKLAND

CATCH ME IF YOU CAN

A Bantam Book / August 1995

*If you would be interested in receiving protective vinyl covers for your
Loveswept books, please write to this address for information:*

Loveswept
Bantam Books
P.O. Box 985
Hicksville, NY 11802

ISBN 0-553-44450-6

Published simultaneously in the United States and Canada

ONE

Abigail Roberts hesitated at the arched opening of the long, dark passageway, peering inside to reassure herself there was light at the other end. The weathered stone was rough and cold beneath her touch, and her head spun with second thoughts about the advisability of what she was about to begin. Riding close cover on those thoughts, however, was the immutable reminder that the first step had long since been taken. The upcoming scene was pivotal, but by no definition could it be called a beginning.

Closure was a more appropriate choice of words. Or, perhaps, the beginning of the end. As such, it would be much more dramatic if played up on the ramparts than amidst the heather and gorse flanking the fort.

Tanner Flynn had always contended it was her sense of style and flair for the unusual that had forced them into adversarial roles. Abby interpreted his appraisal of the situation as a compliment, one she relished even as she strove to convince herself that it was actually Tanner's own ruthless ambition that had driven the wedge between them.

Style had dictated her choice of this lonely fortress for their meeting. Ambition was Tanner's motive for agreeing to come. Those two constants were about to confront each other once again.

She glanced over her shoulder to confirm she was still alone, then took the first steps into the past, ducking her head even though the portal was high enough to accommodate all but the tallest of men. Tanner Flynn was taller than most, and would have to stoop as he traversed the passage.

If tons of rock was what it took to make the man bend, where did she get off thinking she could do the same? Abby knew that she dared because there were no other choices. The part of her life that included Tanner Flynn could only come to an end with his cooperation.

She picked her way between the uneven stones and pools of water that made an obstacle course of the twenty-foot-long passage. The journey lasted mere seconds, but by the time she came out at the other end and stepped into the open-air enclosure, she felt as though she'd traveled centuries. Backward, of course. They didn't build fortifications like this in the space age.

It was called Grianan of Aileach by the Irish, a name that was borderline pronounceable to a woman who spoke Japanese with a Spanish accent and English with the slow, honeyed drawl she'd picked up from her Atlanta-born parents. Abby practiced rolling the name off her tongue as she climbed the narrow steps that led to the top of the circular stone wall, which encompassed an area of about seventy-five feet in diameter. The wind whipped at her short hair in an increasing frenzy, but so absorbed was she in her climb that she hardly noticed.

When she reached the top and caught her first glimpse of the panoramic view that comprised much of County Donegal as well as a goodly portion of Northern Ireland, it occurred to her that the assorted shades of green she'd noticed while driving had been no more than a tiny sample of the full palette. From this hilltop fort, Abby saw more variations on the color green than she'd imagined existed. Lakes the color of robins' eggs dotted the landscape, and tiny villages with churches whose spires reached for the heavens were tucked into the folds of emerald forests and patchwork fields.

Abby decided that it didn't matter how Grianan of Aileach was pronounced. If the words didn't mean "View of the World," it had been misnamed.

The two-thousand-year-old ring fort stood proud and strong at the top of a hill not far from Derry. It was an ancient monument to days long past when walls of rock were meant to withstand the most ferocious of enemies. Well, *most* enemies. Sometime in the twelfth century, she'd read, Murtogh O'Brien—a.k.a. King of Munster—had come along and demolished the fort around the ears of the O'Neills, who had called it their own for around seven hundred years. The fact that Abby was able to stand atop the substantial walls in the late twentieth century was testament to an amateur archaeologist who had reconstructed the whole thing some hundred years earlier.

Something bright flashed at the corner of her vision. Threading the fingers of one hand into the blond curls that lashed at the corners of her eyes, she swung her gaze to the autumn-green fields between which ribboned the dirt road she'd traveled earlier. Silver streaked across a gap in the hedge, then was lost again as the road curled around the hill and out of sight. In much the same way as a marksman takes aim on a moving target, she led with her gaze and was there waiting when an elegant silver sports car broke cover.

From her vantage point, Abby watched the car ease up the last bit of single-track lane and park next to the Vauxhaul she'd rented two days earlier in Dublin. Almost magically, the mud-spattered Vauxhaul assumed an air of careless neglect.

"Trust Tanner to rent a Jaguar," she muttered, pushing her hands deep into the fleece-lined pockets of her pea coat as the driver opened the door and got out. She stayed perfectly still as Tanner straightened to his full height and turned toward the fort. He'd always been a formidable man, but on this remote hillside, he seemed bigger. Stronger.

She wondered if Murtogh O'Brien had been so impressive, if the O'Neills had quaked in their boots at his arrival. And, more pertinently, if Tanner had the slightest clue as to why she'd sent for him.

There was, she mused, always a chance he'd interpret this as a strike instead of the retaliation that she meant for it to appear. Either way, she wasn't bothered. Tanner could think what he wanted. He always had. In any case, it wouldn't be long before he realized it had nothing to do with their private business war at all.

The reason she'd brought Tanner to Ireland was strictly personal.

For a long moment he gazed in her direction, the wind snatching at his open coat and the sun glinting off the mirrored aviator glasses he favored. His shoulder-length dark brown hair whipped at the collar of his coat, and from the colors of his clothing, she guessed he'd dressed for their meeting in faded jeans and a cashmere sweater. Textures were important to Tanner, and the combination of soft denim and the Cadillac of wools was a favorite choice. Her hands curled into fists, and she shivered in her silk blouse and soft wool slacks that suddenly seemed inadequate, even beneath the thick navy wool pea coat.

Tanner lifted a hand and pulled off his glasses, giving Abby an eerie feeling that he was inviting her to look into his soul and know that nothing had changed. The fact that they were separated by more than fifty yards didn't dispel that sensation. Nor did the knowledge that she could be standing toe-to-toe with Tanner and still not see beyond the enigmatic smile and half-shuttered gaze she knew so well.

For several years now she'd had a lot of practice guessing what Tanner Flynn was thinking. Far from being a trivial pursuit, it was a vital element in their ongoing battle. Sometimes she guessed wrong, and the penalties for those errors in judgment had ranged from minor annoyances to heart-stopping crises, such as the one last year that had sent her teetering at the brink of bankruptcy for a long, terrifying week. Her recovery had been equally as spectacular, and contrary to what she knew Tanner had expected, she'd reentered the battle with less caution than ever.

Her reward for guessing right—something she'd gotten better at over the years—was diminished by the knowledge that her victory would be short-lived. Lately, that crumb of glory hadn't been enough to feed her enthusiasm for what was a very demanding business. Desert Reef, the elegant giftware and clothing boutique she owned just down the street from Tanner's Rift—a substantially larger emporium carrying similar merchandise—no longer excited her as it had five years earlier. Deep inside, Abby knew it had nothing to do with the intense competition that had sprung up between her and Tanner the moment she'd first opened her doors for business.

It was time for a change. She wasn't giving up the battle, she reminded herself. She was merely changing the venue. It was, she mused, a bonus that in doing so, she also eliminated Tanner from her list of competitors.

The thought was both comforting and bittersweet. Tanner, for all his arrogant interference, had been a worthy opponent. She would miss him.

Abby narrowed her gaze on the man who had come all the way from Phoenix, Arizona, to meet her and wondered how he would react when he discovered the intimate nature of her personal agenda. Would his dark gaze cloud to conceal his thoughts, or would he listen to her words without so much as a misplaced blink? Would he lose his temper and, if he did, would he let her know it? The possibilities were endless, and every one of them as uninformative as the next. Guesswork would tell her more than any visual hints.

It sometimes astonished Abby that she knew him so well . . . without really knowing him at all. His every expression was as familiar to her as a lover's should be, yet lovers was something they'd never been. Well, not quite. There had been just that once when they'd almost . . . A shudder rippled between her shoulder blades, then repeated when Tanner tossed his glasses into the car and shut the door.

A cloud drifted across the weak November sun, enveloping the hilltop in a chill as Tanner began walking toward the fort. When he went around to the entrance and disappeared from sight, Abby leveled unseeing eyes on the view and wondered if the O'Neills had invited Murtogh inside their defenses as she had invited Tanner inside hers. She doubted it. The battle between the two clans was sure to have been more straightforward than the one between herself and Tanner.

For Abby to win, it was essential to bring him close.

Behind her, she could hear the steady tread of his boots upon the steps. As he climbed and drew closer, her body tensed, preparing for the moment when she would have to turn around and face him. There was a crunch of pebbles not five feet away, and as she began to pivot on the ball of her foot, a strange thing happened: Warmth, gentle and reassuring, blossomed in her chest and spread outward, calming her nerves and bringing a surprised smile to her lips.

Even more surprising was the expression she caught in Tanner's gaze before he shuttered his eyes to her. Abby's smile broadened as she realized she'd seen something he hadn't wanted her to see. The look in his eyes had been one of pure masculine desire. She knew because she'd seen it before—three years earlier in Aspen, Colorado, when he'd taken her to his bed to make love to her.

This wasn't, she realized, going to be quite the uphill battle she'd envisioned. Knowing he still wanted her gave her hope. Still, she wasn't so foolish as to think Tanner would fall in with her wishes without a certain amount of resistance. After all, he'd managed to control his desire for her at a point when most men wouldn't—or couldn't—have bothered trying. He'd lain hard and naked between her thighs . . . and left her without satisfying either of them.

It was time he finished what he'd begun. Perhaps then she could get on with the rest of her life.

Abby narrowed her gaze on the man standing silently before her and thought that he didn't look particularly amenable to rectifying a three-year-old case of coitus interruptus. His mouth was set hard and uncompromising in a face tanned by long days in the sun—he spent most of his free time on his boat, she knew—and lined by forty years of stubbornness and determination.

No matter. She could be just as stubborn. She took a deep breath and opened negotiations. "Glad you made it, Tanner. Grianan of Aileach isn't as well marked as I'd hoped. I went past the turnoff three times before I finally found it." She thought his eyebrows raised a millimeter or so, but she wouldn't swear to it.

"I'm surprised you left the sign in place," he said, his husky voice stoking the warmth building deep inside her. "If my memory serves me correctly, I once lost out on a contract for some rather special pink coral necklaces because you'd gotten there first and turned the sign to point in the opposite direction. I ended up on the wrong side of the island where the coral was substandard and the artisans considerably less skilled."

"If you'd arrived before me, you wouldn't have left a single necklace for me to buy." She crossed her arms and leaned back against the parapet. "That wouldn't have been fair, not when it was I who discovered that village the summer before."

"I had no idea you intended buying a second lot." Tanner moved to lean a hip against the solid wall as he looked down at her, the golden flecks in his hazel eyes shining brighter than she remembered. "You could have warned me."

"Not my job." She cocked her head, delighted because Tanner seemed willing to save the shouting for later. It was, she realized, the first time they'd had a civil discussion in years. Three years, to be precise. She continued. "If your designer hadn't seen the necklaces in *my* boutique window and made the mistake of planning your entire spring line around them, there wouldn't have been a problem."

"The only problem was that you got every artisan in the village to sign an exclusivity clause with you." He lifted a hand to rub the back of his neck as though the memory pained him. "We never did manage to find that particular color of coral anywhere else. Without the necklaces to accessorize, the line lacked any flair whatsoever. It flopped."

"And six months later, I nearly went bankrupt because your overzealous buyers offered outrageous incentives for exclusive contracts with *my* regular suppliers of handmade knits. I had to pay through the nose just to get enough stock to keep the doors open." It was more difficult now to keep her smile in place, but she managed. "I'd say you got better than even, Tanner."

"Perhaps." The hint of a smile tickled one corner of his mouth, and Abby watched, fascinated, as he subdued it. "But you're still one up on me for that trick you pulled in Singapore, or weren't you aware that by canceling my ticket, you stranded me in the path of a nasty little typhoon?"

Her composure cracked slightly, but as he was standing beside her alive and well, she was able to regroup without too much difficulty. The two days of typhoon-enforced communications failure with Singapore had been two of the longest days in her life. She didn't like thinking about them. "If you didn't insist on doing so much of the buying for that oversize store of yours, I wouldn't have to trip you up every now and again."

"At that particular moment, I was headed back to Phoenix."

"By way of Spain," she said, "which was where I'd arranged to meet the artist who did those gorgeous floral triptyches. I couldn't afford to let you get there first."

His gaze was slightly curious. "I never did learn why you came back empty-handed."

"I decided they were ridiculously overpriced." In truth, she'd spent the entire two days sitting in her hotel in front of the TV, too distracted by the danger she'd put Tanner into to shop. By the time the typhoon had passed and she discovered Tanner was en route to Phoenix, the artist had sold the entire collection to a buyer from an exclusive Beverly Hills boutique. She could only hope Tanner never saw them because they were exactly the price and type of merchandise she normally carried.

Abby decided the tit-for-tat trip down memory lane had gone on long enough. They could always resume it later. God knew there was enough material to keep it going long into the night. "Accusing me of even thinking about moving the sign for Grianan of Aileach is illogical. After all, you're here at my invitation."

"I'm here because you told my secretary that if I didn't come, you'd convince the powers that be at the chamber of commerce that I have secret ambitions of becoming mayor." The wind slapped his hair across his eyes, but his gaze didn't waver. "I decided that flying halfway around the world was less trouble than convincing the good civic leaders otherwise. Do you have any idea what they're like once they direct their energies toward the campaign trail?"

"Of course I do. That's why I said it. Besides, Ireland isn't as far from Phoenix as all that."

"It is when you've had to rearrange an already full schedule to get here."

"I've never known you to let your social life interfere with business, Tanner," she said with mocking sweetness, "but, then, Andrea is reputed to be quite a handful. Is there a charity ball or theater opening she'll have to attend all by her lonesome?" At the mention of the year's hottest model whom she'd seen clutching Tanner's arm in several society page photos, his gaze darkened—though whether it was with anger or amusement, she couldn't tell.

"We were discussing why you chose Grianan of Aileach for this meeting, not my social life."

"Maybe I just wanted a piece of neutral ground to give you the good news. I've decided to sell Desert Reef." Her overriding personal motive for bringing him to Ireland would come out later, when . . . *if* she worked up the nerve. There was always a chance he'd be on the next plane back to Phoenix without ever knowing.

For the longest time, the flapping of their coats was the only sound. Then Tanner looked around him and nodded. "You picked a hell of a place for your surrender."

"Interesting choice of words," she murmured, the faint tightening of her jaw hinting at an irritation that surfaced despite her best resolve not to let Tanner goad her. She ignored it. "My surrender. What makes you so sure that's what this is?"

His hesitation—discernible to Abby only because she'd been watching him so closely—told her she was still a few precious steps ahead of him. Her lead wouldn't last long, she knew, but it was a comfort all the same.

He said, "If you wish to view the sale of your business as anything less than complete surrender, then that's your prerogative."

"Surrender is what happens between a man and a woman who no longer feel the need for defenses between them," she said a bit more heatedly than she'd intended, then held her breath as she awaited his reply.

The hesitation was there again, longer this time, but less reliable as a meter of her success. The intimate aspect of her comment had narrowed her advantage to a mere breath.

"Your knowledge of what happens between lovers is appallingly inaccurate," he said softly, and though she could have sworn he didn't move, he seemed closer than he had been just moments ago.

It took all her courage to reply. "And whose fault is that?"

He tilted his head to the side, and the smile that had threatened earlier pushed at the corners of his mouth. "Is that why you've dragged me across an ocean, Abby? To punish me, in some way, for refusing to take your virginity?"

Punish. The word annoyed her, just as his use of surrender had. His broadening smile didn't help either. Her anger at his rejection, which was never far away, surfaced and exploded in a sudden denial of everything she'd thought she wanted—everything, including Tanner and the emotions he fired within her. She'd been mad to even consider it!

She spun on her heel and would have run were it not for the strong masculine hand catching her arm. When she jerked her head up to share a good portion of that anger with him, he quieted her with two fingers across her lips. His smile was gone now, replaced by a thoughtful expression she couldn't remember seeing before.

"What's the matter, Abby? Still haven't forgiven me?"

"Forgive has nothing to do with it," she said, her lips moving against his fingers until he slid his hand to the side of her face. Her anger melted at his strangely comforting gesture. "It's forgetting that I'm having trouble with. I had this wild idea you could help me past that, but I must have been suffering from delusions brought on by persistent nightmares of a hungry Great Dane snapping at my heels."

The barest hint of amusement glimmered in his eyes. "A Great Dane?" he said softly. "You must wake up screaming."

"Luckily, I'm smarter and faster than the brute." She was on the verge of nuzzling deeper into the warm strength of his hand, but years of practiced aloofness kept her still.

He gave an abrupt laugh, and his hand tensed against her face. "Abby, lass, how could I possibly help you to forget when every time I see you, I remember that night as though it were yesterday? If only you hadn't been a virgin—"

"Would it make a difference now?" she asked. "I mean, if I wasn't—"

Anger, dark and menacing, flared in his eyes and stayed there. It occurred to her that she'd seen and understood more emotion in him that afternoon than she had in the five years since they'd first met.

"I take that to mean you finally found someone who had no scruples about taking your virginity." He jerked his hand from her face as though it were on fire. "Congratulations, Abby. I hope that particular rite of passage was everything you expected."

"What *is* it with you, Tanner?" Her fingernails bit deep into her palms as her hands fisted at her sides. "First, you won't make love to me—"

"I know it's been three years, but I seem to remember doing just that—at least up to the point when you sprang your little surprise on me." He took several agitated strides in the opposite direction before spinning around to face her. "You could have warned me it was your first time! I wouldn't have let it go so far."

She continued as though she hadn't heard him. "You wouldn't make love to me then because of some passé moralistic stand that prevents you from deflowering virgins, and now you're angry because you think someone else took what you refused. Is there no pleasing you?"

"What do you mean, because *I* think someone else took what I refused? Isn't that what you just told me?"

"I said *if* I wasn't—"

"Are you or are you not a virgin?" he demanded hotly.

"I'm beginning to think it doesn't make a difference!" she shouted.

A sudden stillness overtook him. "You're right. It doesn't make any difference at all."

"I see." Allowing herself to believe he wanted her for anything but a sparring partner had been sheer fantasy on her part. Disappointment ripped her anger into unrecognizable shreds, but dignity—always a handy disguise—came to the rescue. "All of this is beside the point, of course. I didn't bring you here to discuss my personal life."

He didn't look as though he believed her, but he let it go. "You sent for me to give me first option on Desert Reef, right?"

"Wrong."

He frowned. "You're not offering it to me?"

"Don't be silly, Tanner. The last thing you need is a miniature version of your own business. I suspect that if you did make an offer, it would be only so that you could close it down—and you'd be stupid to pay what I'm asking just for that privilege."

"Then why am I here?"

"Like I said, I just wanted to give you the good news in person. As for Ireland, let's say I owed you a bit of inconvenience for that stunt your buyer Samuels pulled in Scotland." Retaliation, she reminded herself, was something they could both relate to. They'd certainly had enough practice.

"He isn't—" Tanner began, then his eyes narrowed and he asked something altogether different. "What did Samuels do to you?"

"Another time, Tanner. I need to get on the road before it rains." *And before I completely and totally fall apart.* Abby shook her head in an effort to clear it of unproductive thoughts.

"I want to know now," he said.

"Trust me, Tanner, it was enough to warrant your trek to this fort. Ask Samuels about it when you get back. I'm sure he'll be able to reassure you."

"Tell me, Abby," he said, his voice dangerously

soft. "Is what Samuels did responsible for your decision to sell?"

"No!" She shook her head tiredly, wanting to rub the ache in her temple but not caring to let Tanner know she was hurting. "Samuels has nothing to do with it, not really. I've been thinking about getting into something else, and the perfect opportunity came up last month. I need to sell, though, before I can move on."

"You're leaving Phoenix then," he said, and there was a curious deadness about the way he said it.

She didn't answer because she wasn't sure yet about that part of it. "If you're miffed because I haven't given you a chance at Desert Reef, then get in line with Sandra Harringdon," she said, naming a mutual acquaintance from Scottsdale. "She's been interested ever since she saw that load of native jewelry I picked up in South America last year. Actually, she was even more impressed by the emerald earrings I'd bought for myself on the same trip, but when I told her how much duty I'd had to pay, she agreed gems weren't worth the hassle."

"And she's the only one interested?"

"The only one I'm taking seriously. There's Yoshimoto, but I won't sell to him." The youngish Japanese man was new to the Scottsdale business community, but had managed to wedge himself fairly deeply within it by buying into a computer retail chain based in Phoenix. He'd been after Abby for months now to sell Desert Reef to him—long before she'd decided that was what she wanted to do. His offers had slid gradually from honest stock-for-stock trades as bonuses, downward into the realm of tax-free incentives in the form of under-the-table cash.

Lately, he'd resorted to slapping contracts onto her desk accompanied by badly disguised threats against her person. His thuglike style was so out of place in her world that she couldn't take him seriously. On the other hand, neither did she feel like sticking around Phoenix for more of the same. Until contracts had been exchanged with Sandra, she intended to stay as far away as possible.

"Why not Yoshimoto?" Tanner asked. "He seems to be loaded, if it's money you're after."

Skirting the whole truth, she said quite honestly, "There's something about Yoshimoto that puts me off."

"What?"

"Maybe I just don't like the fact he won't take no for an answer." She shrugged off the nervous sensation she always got these days when thinking about the Japanese executive. "In any case, the numbers Sandra has come up with so far are better than anything Yoshimoto ever offered me. If you're interested, think big."

He studied her for a moment, then shook his head. "You were right about why I'd buy Desert Reef. If you're happy with Sandra's offer, you should take it."

"I intend to." She was curious about his easy acceptance of continued competition. "You don't look worried about having Sandra take up the battle."

"I'm not. I've seen her café on Fifth Avenue, and it's nothing special. Without your buying instincts, the competition won't be nearly as fierce."

"Then we both win for a change, don't we?"

He again hesitated for a moment. Abby could have sworn he was going to disagree with her, but he just said, "So what are you going to be doing with all that excess energy of yours? I can't imagine you retiring to the porch swing, at least not for another hundred years or so."

"Actually, I'm buying into a travel business. It occurred to me a while back that the part I liked best about Desert Reef was the traveling around, so I decided to concentrate on that and give up the rest." It was also fitting, she'd thought, that the money from the trust fund she'd tapped to open Desert Reef would now roll over into the kind of business that people like her parents relied on so heavily. With a little luck and some minor arm-twisting, she might even pick up their account. That alone should keep her in cornflakes for the foreseeable future.

Tanner cocked his head and regarded her curiously. "You want to travel more? I should hardly think that's possible. I think I saw you more on the road last year than in Phoenix."

"It's not so much that I'll travel more," she said, a touch defensively although she couldn't imagine what she had to be defensive about. "I just want to enjoy the trips I do take—without having to spend all my time looking over my shoulder."

When he didn't reply to that, she turned and headed toward the nearest set of steps. As she descended to the fort's grassy floor, she heard the sounds of Tanner trailing after her. He stayed there, behind her, as she negotiated the tunnel. Once outside the thick walls, she neither slowed nor hurried her pace, determined as she was not to let his presence influence her in any way.

She ignored him, because it was the only way she knew of keeping her fragile mantle of dignity from shattering. He was behind her, and she pretended he wasn't . . . which didn't explain why she was so surprised when he placed a restraining hand over hers just as she was pulling the car door open.

"Where are you staying?" His gaze was as dark and unpredictable as the clouds that swirled above.

"Why?"

"So I'll know where to head if I lose you. I'd rather not leave the Jaguar parked here if I can help it."

Irritation mingled with confusion, and she knew they both showed in her expression. "I'm not going your way, Tanner. Now I'd suggest you head back to Dublin and turn in that fancy car before it gets struck by lightning."

"What's the matter, Abby? Lose your nerve?"

"I didn't—"

"You didn't bring me all the way to Ireland just so you could remind me of what an ass I was three years ago," he said before she could get a word in edgewise. "And I certainly didn't come here only to have you send me packing before we'd settled things."

"*How much more settled can things get?*" She realized she was shouting . . . and that it felt good. "I could have sworn I heard you say you wouldn't make love to me regardless of the state of my virginity."

"I never said anything of the kind." He glanced over his shoulder toward where they'd been standing atop the fort, then looked back at her. "What I *did* say was that it no longer made a difference."

"Oh." She swallowed hard, thinking that losing her nerve might serve her better than going ahead with this insane idea.

"Now where's that hotel?"

Nonplussed, she named a small town about an hour northeast of Donegal. She wasn't, she told herself, committing to anything. If Tanner wanted to follow her across Ireland, that was his decision. She could go on pretending that night in Aspen had never happened. She might even forget about it altogether, now that they wouldn't have the excuse of business to keep them in each other's company.

"I saw a phone box at the bottom of the hill," he said. "Call ahead and get me a room for the night while I look at the map."

Tanner's spin on events kept her from voicing any but the most insignificant of details. "I thought you grew up over here. What do you need with a map?"

"I left when I was but a lad of sixteen." There was a beguiling lilt in his voice that she'd never heard before. "My memory of out-of-the-way towns isn't all that it used to be."

"Senility before forty?" she drawled. "What a shame."

"I was forty last year, but don't let it worry you. I'm sure I can manage to keep up with you."

"I never doubted that for a second, Tanner." She patted the hood of the rented Vauxhaul. "The tiny engine in this thing doesn't stand a chance against your Jag."

Humor softened his gaze. "Now about that room . . ."

She was at once disappointed and relieved that he'd detoured past the intimate dialogue. "It's not your typical tourist haunt, Tanner. It's more of a country house turned hotel, the kind of place people go for a quiet weekend. They're probably already booked for the night."

"I doubt it."

Abby opened her mouth to argue further, but he

silenced her as effectively as he'd done on the hill with the same two fingers across her lips. She sensed that he was, this time, substantially more resolved that she pay attention.

"Get me a room or plan on sharing yours, Abby," he said in a low, steady voice as his fingers slipped away. "I'm not going back to Phoenix without settling this once and for all."

"There's nothing left to settle."

"In that case, it won't take very long, will it?"

TWO

If Tanner stayed closer to the Vauxhaul's rear bumper than was strictly necessary for someone who had a fair idea of where he was going, it was because he didn't trust Abby not to make a break for it. Given the opportunity, he guessed she'd leave him stuck behind a hay wagon or at one of the rare stoplights and disappear. As she'd neglected to give him the name of the hotel, he thought it prudent to keep her in sight. Therefore, each time she pulled out to pass another vehicle, he did the same. When she put on her turn signal, he was just as prepared to go the opposite direction—which was good because she pulled that trick twice in Letterkenny.

It was, he mused, also a good thing he'd rented the Jaguar. Abby's special brand of cunning was already more than enough to keep him alert. If she'd rented a car with a bigger engine, she might well have succeeded in losing him.

Why she wanted to do so annoyed him more than he cared to admit. It wasn't like Abby to back away from anything, yet Tanner had stood on the ramparts and watched her backpedal for all she was worth. He hadn't for a second believed that her real purpose in bringing him all the way from Phoenix was to retaliate for whatever had happened in Scotland—which left the unfinished business between them as the only viable explanation.

It was about time.

Without taking his eyes off the red Vauxhaul ahead, he replayed their conversation and wondered what had angered her more—his tactless remarks about the current status of her virginity or the way he'd equated her decision to sell with giving up. A grimace creased his face, and he swore loud and without inhibition. As he had on that night three years earlier, he'd handled things badly.

He could, he supposed, blame his clumsiness on surprise, but that was a lousy excuse. After all, he'd waited a long time for her to refer to what had happened between them, not knowing for certain if she ever would, but hoping all the same. He'd been tempted a hundred times to say something himself, but never did, reasoning that he owed her the courtesy of pretending the incident had never happened if that was her wish.

His silence on the subject had been matched by hers. Away from Phoenix, their paths often crossed, a consequence of their competitive natures as well as Tanner's curious need to see her. While she didn't go out of her way to avoid him, he always felt as though she was on the verge of bolting. At home, there were numerous occasions when they were thrown together, what with all the cocktail parties and dinners they regularly attended as members of a tight-knit business community. Still, Aspen and all that had happened between them there remained an ignored issue.

All she would have had to do was indicate with a smile or a look that she wanted to talk privately, and it would have been a simple matter to arrange. God knew how many untried scenarios for a discreet escape he'd scrapped because Abby hadn't given him so much as a hint that she would leave with him if he asked. Instead, she'd kept their conversations on a business level—if recounting the latest round of dirty tricks could be considered business.

Tanner would have believed she'd forgotten that night entirely were it not for the fact that she never quite looked him in the eye.

Exhaling a long breath, he thought that a man who wanted something to happen shouldn't be taken by surprise when it finally did, but Abby's softly spoken words had thrown him off center, and he'd been unprepared for what had followed.

Surrender is what happens between a man and a woman who no longer feel the need for defenses between them.

As far as Tanner was concerned, surrender implied compliance, even subservience. He didn't want that from any woman, and particularly not from Abby. He wanted her to give, not forfeit. He wanted her to lower her defenses without feeling defenseless.

He wanted to dance the lovers' waltz with her without feeling he was taking something she might regret giving. That was why he'd stopped a hair's breadth from finishing what he'd begun that night in Aspen. Until that moment, the fact that he might be her first lover had never occurred to him.

A smile softened his features as he placed the blame for that particular misunderstanding on Abby's doorstep. She'd been a flirt who didn't tease, a seductress without wiles. Her smoky gray eyes had featured in dreams that were a beguiling combination of gaiety and erotica, and the hint of Southern honey in her voice was like a caress on his senses.

Physically, she was the exact opposite of the type of woman he normally kept company with. Tanner had always sought out women who were fairly tall and didn't look so fragile that he worried he might break them. Brunettes had always attracted him more than blondes or redheads, and silky, long hair that fanned luxuriously across his pillow was a sensual delight. The women he'd felt most at ease with were generally reserved and always sophisticated.

Abby was a small woman, nearly a foot shorter than his own six feet. Her hair was also short—not to mention blond and curly—and she had a youthful vivaciousness that made the air around her seem to spark and sizzle. There was nothing reserved in the way she faced life, and her only sophistication was the ability to go anywhere and do anything without being intimidated by the unknown.

Tanner had been intrigued by her charming combination of innocence and daring, so much so that the women in his life had soon begun to resemble indistinguishable stereotypes. Abby had never been predictable or boring, and if she frequently irritated him, she made up for it by being a gracious loser when circumstances warranted.

Except for once, when in a single act of childish reprisal, she'd put into motion events that had changed both their lives. On that cold, wintry night in Aspen, the snowball she'd pitched as he walked from his chalet to the hotel had caught him square in the back of his neck. He'd retaliated without hesitation, throwing one straight back at her. And the fight was on.

Tanner had recognized the attack as nothing more than Abby's way of letting him know how annoyed she was with him for beating her out of some particularly fine quilts. He'd known that, and still hadn't been able to back away when the fight was over and they were both covered in snow. Huge clumps of it were plastered to their coats, tangled in their hair. Laughing and breathless, she'd followed him into the light where he could see well enough to brush the snow away.

Just when his touch changed from task to caress he wasn't certain. It simply happened, both of them noticing but neither daring to say a word. She just looked up at him with her eyes bright and excited and her lips parted and trembling as he bent his head to taste her innocent arousal.

That night in Aspen, he'd taken Abby to his bed because it had seemed the right thing to do. He'd stopped short of taking her virginity for the same reason. For three years, Tanner had believed he'd made the right decision.

His rage at learning that another man had taken what he'd refused had surprised him as much as it obviously had Abby. He shouldn't have reacted that way, he knew, not in a modern world where a woman's virginity was supposedly no more or less sacred than a man's. It was just that the image of Abby with her arms and legs wrapped around another man was one he'd never quite come to terms with. He'd known she must have taken lovers, but having her say it aloud had, somehow, made it more real.

He wondered if her first lover had been gentle and understanding . . . and if Abby had come apart in his arms with the same joyful abandon she'd exhibited in Tanner's.

The rain that had been threatening all afternoon hit without the preamble of gentle drops. Within seconds, the Jaguar was engulfed in a deluge and Tanner was forced to slow. For a moment, he worried that Abby would take the opportunity to try to lose him. The Vauxhaul slowed, though, and he breathed a quiet thanks that she'd allowed her common sense to overcome her panic. From all the warning signs he'd noticed along the way, the narrow, winding road that led north from Letterkenny had a track record that wasn't kind to risk takers. At times it seemed more of a path than a road, alternating between dark claustrophobic tunnels created by the clutching branches of large trees and short sprints in the open that paralleled the shore and mushroom-gray waters of Lough Swilly.

He settled back against the leather-cushioned seat and detoured his thoughts to Scotland and whatever Samuels had done there. Years ago when a rumor had reached him about how Tanner's buyers were imitating their boss and playing tricks on Abby in their efforts to beat her to merchandise, Tanner had made it clear there were only two players in that game: Himself and Abby.

Obviously, Samuels hadn't believed him—a serious lapse that would, in normal circumstances, have cost him his job. As things stood now, Tanner would first have to discover what Samuels had done before he could decide what to do about it. If the incident turned out to have been more than a simple inconvenience, he would give Samuels cause to regret his behavior.

No one hurt Abby and got away with it.

Not even Tanner.

Their destination was Rathmullan, a small town perched on the western shore of Lough Swilly—an inlet that cut into the northernmost reaches of the Republic of Ireland. The rain had stopped by the time they arrived there, and in the murky half-light of a typical November afternoon, the cars glided one behind the other through the village's narrow streets. Tanner's feeling that Abby knew where she was going without benefit of road signs was confirmed by the way she drove without hesitation straight through the town and beyond. Minutes later, she turned down a long, rutted drive and followed it to the end where a magnificent white-painted mansion rose proud and serene amidst a landed sea of green lawns and gardens.

Abby gave Tanner no time to admire the two-story structure with its triple set of bay windows. She drove straight into the parking lot hidden around back, then disappeared inside before he'd retrieved his leather case from the Jaguar's trunk. Pausing, Tanner debated whether to disable her car, but decided against it . . . for the moment. He could always sneak out later and take care of it.

He didn't expect Abby to be waiting for him inside, so he wasn't disappointed that she wasn't there. He was greeted, instead, by an atmosphere of elegance and a stylishly dressed woman who invited him into the reception office where he learned that Abby had managed to reserve him accommodations of his own. When they'd left Grianan of Aileach, Abby had used the phone box at the bottom of the hill, but she could have as easily called the local police to complain that a man was stalking her, as she could have called the hotel. He was relieved she'd done the latter. He also learned which room Abby herself was in, information easily gained as the woman assumed Abby wouldn't have brought him there if she wanted to avoid him.

Suitcase in hand, Tanner mounted the wide staircase to the second floor. He passed Abby's door on the way to his own room and was about to knock when her door swung open. Her hair was a windblown mass of curls that she obviously hadn't bothered trying to tame, and she still wore outdoor clothing.

"I'm going for a walk on the beach," she said.

"Sounds great. Just let me dump my suitcase—"

"You're not invited."

It didn't seem like a good idea to let her go alone, not if he wanted to make sure she was still around for dinner. He put his suitcase down on the thick carpet. "If it's privacy you're after, I promise to stay ten paces behind you."

"Thanks, but I've had you behind me long enough today already." She blew the hair from her eyes in a show of frustration. The golden curls lifted for a short moment, then fell back into place, neatly obscuring her gaze from his. "If you want to walk, you'll have to go by yourself."

"I don't know the way to the beach." He would have missed the fleeting upward tilt of her mouth if he hadn't been watching.

"It's at the edge of the water," she said. "Don't worry, Tanner. I'm only going for a walk. This is the best hotel in the area, and I'm not letting you chase me out of it."

"Then it must have been my imagination that you tried to lose me on the road."

"Must have been," she agreed. "If I'd wanted to shake you off, you wouldn't be standing here now."

"It bruises my ego to admit you might have succeeded doing so in a car with a bigger engine. I remember that time in Palermo when you offered to let me follow you so I wouldn't get lost on the way to dinner."

Not long after Abby had opened Desert Reef, she and Tanner had been part of a merchant group from Phoenix that had been invited by the Italians to tour Sicily for the purpose of boosting that island's exports. The dinner party Tanner referred to had been at a villa outside of town, and when Tanner had offered to drive Abby, she'd declined with the excuse that she intended to make an overnight trip to Erice after dinner. As everyone else had already left and she was in possession of the last hand-drawn map, she had offered to let him follow.

She'd managed to lose him in the suburbs of Palermo, and it had taken him three hours and a very embarrassing phone call to find the villa. The memory of his hosts' annoyance at what they clearly deemed a deliberate discourtesy still chafed.

She said, "I've always wondered where you disappeared to that night. One moment you were there behind me, and the next you were gone."

"If you hadn't been so anxious to get to Erice, I would have told you that night what I thought of your driving."

"Thank you. A compliment delayed is still a compliment."

Her smile hinted again, but she ducked her head and by the time she'd pulled the door closed, it was gone. Tanner stepped backward and wasn't surprised when she took advantage of the opportunity to bolt down the stairs and out the front door. Through the windows on either side, he watched as she struck out across the front lawn and disappeared into the thick shrubbery.

She was either going to the beach or taking the long way around to the parking lot. While he wanted to believe her, there was a history between them that urged caution. Without any serious second thoughts, he went into her room—easy enough to do because none of the doors had keys, just dead bolts on the inside to keep intruders out while you slept.

Tanner checked the surfaces until he spotted her car keys atop a polished secretary over by the window. Just to make sure she hadn't planted a red herring, he checked the tag against the Vauxhaul's registration plates. He had memorized the plates after following Abby's car for an hour. They matched. For whatever reason, Abby was apparently staying a while longer.

As a precaution, Tanner slipped the keys into his pocket and had started to leave the room when he spotted a door cut into the wall adjoining the next room—*his* room, unless he was very much mistaken. There was a smile on his face as he crossed to it and slid open the dead bolt, then left Abby's room.

He wasn't mistaken. Tanner picked up his bag and walked into the room adjoining Abby's. It was similar to hers—a suite, really, with a comfortably furnished sitting area in the bay window, a good-sized bed that looked like it had been built to accommodate men of his height, and a huge bathroom with sparkling fixtures. He went around the bed to the connecting door, and with a flick of his wrist, shot back the dead bolt. When he tried the handle, the door opened into Abby's room without so much as a telltale squeak. He closed it and hoped that Abby wouldn't think to check the lock.

He wanted to have a private chat with her before dinner, and cornering her seemed to be the only way he was going to accomplish that.

First, though, he had to wait for her to return. Tanner walked over to the bay windows which gave an excellent view of the spot where Abby had disappeared. Pouring himself a glass of mineral water from the bottle on the dresser, he settled down to wait. He could, he realized, have just as easily gone after her, but the only good that would have done would be to reassure him. He figured he needed reassurance less than Abby needed time alone.

There was a leather-bound folder on the coffee table, and Tanner glanced through it in between long looks outside. He checked the dinner hour, saw that there was a bar in the cellar which would be open soon, and read the blurb, which compressed two centuries of Rathmullan House's history into a single incomprehensible paragraph.

When he checked his watch, he saw that a mere five minutes had passed since Abby had disappeared down the path. It seemed an eternity.

"Whoever said that the passage of time was a constant should be taken out and shot." He was surprised that having expressed his frustration aloud, he felt somewhat better.

He would have felt even better if time had bent to his will and flown by, but it didn't happen, so he spent the eternity considering those things he had a real chance of affecting.

❖━━━━❖

The sun's rays were slanted almost horizontally as Abby paused beneath one of the three enormous willows that graced the hotel's front lawn. She disregarded the waning light as having any real bearing on the time, then checked her watch for confirmation. It was hardly four o'clock, yet her emotions agreed with the sun that the day had gone on long enough. So much had happened, and it wasn't even time for dinner.

Her stomach growled, reminding her that she'd been too nervous to eat breakfast or lunch. Perhaps that was why she hadn't been able to organize her thoughts well enough to do anything useful with them, she mused. Starvation of the brain. An hour on the beach and nothing to show for it except for a perfectly formed starfish she'd found beside a piece of driftwood. She guessed the starfish had attached itself to the wood out of a misguided sense of needing something more solid to hold on to than the shifting ocean floor.

Abby recognized that stability had a certain appeal for some. As far as she was concerned, though, it seduced the unwary with promises of dependability and predictability, then shrouded everything in an impenetrable blanket of boredom.

She knew she had her parents to thank for her appetite for travel and adventure. It was, after all, the way she'd been raised, with a bilingual dictionary in one hand, a suitcase in the other, and her passport clenched between her teeth as she ran alongside her parents to catch the plane or train or ferry. Her father had been something of a troubleshooter for the State Department, called in by this ambassador or that president to ease tensions somewhere in the world before they got bad enough to demand front-page attention.

Her mother had loved the diplomatic life and was

as much of a healer as her husband, working with spouses and aides to repair frayed tempers from the inside out. Her abilities to soothe and regenerate made her husband's job easier, so much so that they were often on their way to the next trouble spot long before Abby had learned to find her way to the bathroom in the dead of night.

By the time she was a teenager, she'd long since realized that her parents' marriage owed its success to interdependence as much as it did to love . . . and that it had nothing to do with where they happened to be. So long as they were together, they were happy.

Most important, they were never, ever bored.

Glancing up at the brilliant white facade of Rathmullan House, Abby knew that boredom was something Tanner Flynn wouldn't tolerate. It was what had attracted her to him in the first place, the feeling that he was in business because he found it exciting and not because he had a driving need to make money. He might be seen by some—including herself at times—as ruthless in his ambitions, but that was likely because he threw everything he had into his business and loved the competition.

It wasn't winning that mattered. The financial reward of besting someone in business was simply a way of keeping score. The contest was all he cared about . . . which was why her five years in direct competition with Tanner had seemed more like a war than a professional rivalry.

It was a war she'd found herself enjoying without quite understanding why, although she knew more or less when her pleasure had begun. It had happened during a rare, quiet moment, an afternoon's pause in Tahiti when they'd been caught in the same beachfront café by a heavy rain shower. Over fruit juice and biscuits, he'd asked her about Desert Reef . . .

"You have to admit, Abby, that Desert Reef is an unusual name," he said, sipping the sweet juice through a long straw. "Tell me about it."

Abby had been annoyed, at first, that he had followed her inside the café when the heavens had opened up, especially after that frantic bidding session they'd just finished at a local pottery workshop. But now, it seemed as though he was making an effort to be civil. She decided she could manage the same.

"Desert Reef makes perfect sense to me," she said. "A reef is the part of the ocean where all the interesting bits collect, which is the kind of merchandise I specialize in. Frankly, it makes a lot more sense than Tanner's Rift."

He grinned and disagreed with a shake of his head. "Not if you equate rift to challenge or struggle. When I first came to Phoenix with my father, we didn't have much more than the clothes on our backs. Everything was a struggle. Building Tanner's Rift into something special was my biggest challenge."

"Was?" she asked, aware of a sudden change in his demeanor.

"Was," he said softly. "I hadn't met you then . . ."

Abby looked down at the starfish in her hand and wondered how she'd segued from theorizing about its demise all the way to the battle between Tanner's Rift and Desert Reef. Then again, there was really no reason to question why she was thinking about Tanner. He was in her thoughts almost constantly these days, and the simple transition of starfish to Tanner was no more unusual than the way bing cherries reminded her of that morning in Honolulu when he'd—

She was doing it again! With an abrupt shake of her head, Abby resumed walking across the lawn. The starfish probably hadn't given any thought at all to the consequences of attaching itself to wood, she realized, then wondered if that by dwelling on the starfish's unfortunate circumstances, she was seeking a parallel to explain her own hopes and dreams.

If so, the parallel was more than a stretch because, contrary to the starfish, she'd thought of nothing *but* the consequences when she'd challenged Tanner with the unfinished business between them. Yet today as she'd stood toe-to-toe with him atop Grianan of Aileach, the ultimate reward of being able to finally put the past behind her had dimmed in importance. Excuses and rationale had been replaced by the undeniable fact that she wanted to make love with Tanner because she'd never in her life experienced such excitement and joy as she had that night in his arms.

Even though it had been her first experience in intimacy, Abby had been neither embarrassed nor shy when Tanner's hot gaze had covered her nakedness and his erotic suggestions had filled her ears. Any worries that her lack of experience would disappoint him had disappeared in the wake of his obvious pleasure. She'd touched him in wonder, and he'd responded with moans and shudders and no attempt whatsoever to hide his pleasure. With his mouth, he'd opened whole new worlds of sensation that were enhanced by his hot words of praise. Her body had been slick with sweat and screaming for release when he'd come to the barrier of her maidenhead.

Abby felt the pulsing heat of embarrassment in her

cheeks as she realized how easily her body responded even now to what was only a memory. It was why, she realized, she'd never been able to get beyond a few innocent kisses with any of the men she'd dated since that night.

Tanner had found in her a depth of passion that had proven to be unresponsive to anyone else. For three years, her body had ached for release while her mind had sought to forget. It had been only recently that she'd come to realize that one depended on the other. For her to be able to respond sexually to another man, she needed to forget Tanner. To forget Tanner, her body had to stop wanting him.

Stepping out of the cold afternoon's embrace and into the deserted foyer, Abby reminded herself it was just her bad fortune that putting theory into action was more unnerving than she'd expected. And, second thoughts or no, it appeared that Tanner had arrived with his own agenda.

For a brief instant, Abby felt the shifting sands beneath her feet . . . and almost found herself wishing for something solid to hold on to.

From the bay window above the door, Tanner watched Abby cross the lawn toward the house. Even from a distance, her cheeks looked as though they'd been brushed raw by the same cold wind that whipped at her curls and forced her to tuck her chin deep inside her heavy anorak.

The next time he saw her, her chin was deep in bubbles and she was wearing no more than a look of stunned disbelief.

THREE

Abby had a kind of love/hate relationship with bathtubs. She loved soaking for hours in hot, scented water. If it was a presleep bath, she'd keep the water nearly scalding until it was time to dry off and climb naked between the cool cotton sheets of her bed. If she was bathing prior to going out, she would let the water gradually cool, and feel totally refreshed when she got out to dress. The tub in her home was a standard size that nicely accommodated her short stature by allowing her to lie down with her head pillowed on a towel and her feet braced against the other end for balance.

Hotel tubs were almost invariably disappointing. Some hotels—for safety reasons, they claimed—put abrasive strips along the bottom. Abby hated those strips, and refused to bathe in any tub that was so decorated. Rathmullan House had not committed that particular sin. Instead, they provided a slip-proof mat—which she elected not to use as she preferred the sleek sensation of porcelain under her bottom to the clingy-but-safe mat.

Unfortunately, they'd erred in another direction. The bathtub was much larger than standard, a luxurious model to be sure, but a definite problem for a woman who barely topped five feet. Abby was only able to keep her head above water by alternately holding on to the edge with her hands or lobbing one leg over the side and letting water drip all over the floor.

She had just settled her leg over the side and her head on a folded towel when a knock sounded at the door. She didn't even flinch—partly because she'd been expecting Tanner but mostly because she'd had the good sense to lock the door. He'd just have to wait until dinner if he wanted to see her. She was wondering whether her nerve was sufficiently restored for her to resume her game plan when she thought she heard the soft whoosh of an opening door. She rolled her head sideways just as Tanner's tall form filled the bathroom doorway. He looked quite at ease as he propped one shoulder against the doorjamb and studied her from behind his shuttered gaze.

Several things happened simultaneously. Her jaw dropped open in stunned amazement, her leg slipped from its perch, and Tanner said, "Hi, Abby." The "Abby" part was a little blurred, because the laws of physics had raced into play and were dragging her under the water before he'd finished speaking. Water and rose-scented suds filled her mouth, and if she hadn't been so incredibly furious, she might have stayed underwater and drowned—just to pay him back for sneaking up on her!

Abby broke the surface as huge hands curled around her arms and began to pull her up. She struggled and won—thanks in no small part to her soap-slickened skin—and felt a surge of satisfaction when the resulting tidal wave drenched Tanner. Crouching behind the solid wall of the tub, she watched as he rocked on his heels and lost his balance to sprawl backward onto the tile floor.

She spat a stream of bath water onto his shoes and swiped the wet curls from her eyes. "What the hell do you think you're doing in here, Tanner Flynn?"

"Trying to keep you from drowning." He eased himself up onto one elbow and blotted the water from his face with his forearm. "Next time I'll leave you to save yourself."

"I would have been fine if you hadn't broken in here and scared me half to death."

"I didn't break in. The door was unlocked."

"You're in the adjoining room?"

He shook his head. "I believe they call it a connecting room when the locks are off. Technically, it would only be adjoining if you locked me out."

"It never occurred to me to request that they put you at the other end of the hotel when I called *or* to check the door in case some lecher decided to pay a visit." She scowled at him over the porcelain rim. "You should have taken the hint that I didn't want any company when you knocked and I didn't answer."

"I was never good at hints." He jackknifed into a sitting position and rested his arm on a raised knee, a move that brought him close enough to make Abby sink a little lower. "Never mind that, though. I came over to talk, not to argue. What do you say, Abby? Truce?"

She felt her eyes go round in disbelief. "It doesn't occur to you that perhaps it might be more appropriate to wait until I'm finished with my bath?"

"No."

"No? What do you mean, no?"

"Just no." There was a strange tension behind the mild tone he used. "There are things we need to say to each other—"

She interrupted. "We can talk at dinner."

"Not with any degree of privacy."

"Then go away until I get dressed. We can talk in my room. Your room. Whichever."

He caught her gaze and smiled. "You walked away from me this afternoon when things got too sticky for you. You'll think twice before you do it now."

She shook her head in frustration, splattering water on him in the process. "Get out of here, Tanner."

"Not until you tell me why you brought me to Ireland."

Her fingers were nearly bloodless from gripping the tub and the water was cooling, but neither discomfort bothered her as much as the idea that she looked like a drowned rat. It wasn't exactly the image one presented to a man one wished to seduce.

Abby decided it was Tanner's fault that everything was going so wrong, and glared at him without speaking.

After what seemed an eternity, he said, "Okay, lass, if that's the way you feel, I'll do the talking."

"I'd rather you left."

"I know, but I can't. Not just yet."

"Why?"

"Because I've been waiting three years for you to give me permission to finish what I couldn't that night in Aspen. I think that's what you were trying to do this afternoon." He looked down at his hands for a moment, then renewed his study of her face. "If I'm wrong, if that's not the reason you brought me to Ireland, then tell me now and I'll go."

Wild panic flared deep inside, but she smothered it with the blanket of temptation, woven from the way he had reduced the situation to the essential facts. After all, she *had* lured him here for that very reason. Being coy about it wouldn't serve her purpose at all. It was just that there was such a huge difference between thinking about doing something and actually doing it. . . . Suddenly, she was struck by the other thing he'd said.

"What do you mean, you've been waiting for permission?"

A grim smile edged his lips. "Exactly that. I'm not so arrogant as to assume you'd be willing to give me another chance just because I'd changed my mind."

"And just when, precisely, did that happen?"

His smile disappeared so completely, Abby thought she'd imagined it. "About two minutes after you slammed out of the chalet."

"I would have felt better knowing that," she murmured. "I never did understand—"

He interrupted with a soft reminder. "Abby, you were about to tell me if I've guessed right about why you brought me to Ireland."

"I was?" She couldn't think why she should have to, not when it was so difficult to get her mouth around the words she wouldn't even need to say if things had ended differently between them that night in Aspen.

"Mm-hmm." Without looking away, he yanked a thick white towel from the heated rack on the wall beside him and used it to blot the water from his face and shirt. "I suppose we could get on with it without all this discussion, but frankly, lass, I don't know how far we'd get before I started wondering if you were looking for an opportunity to get even with me."

"Get even?" She stared at him without the slightest clue what he was talking about.

"Mmm. I can see how you might think it would serve me right to let me get as far as I did last time, then change your mind. Of course, there's always the chance that this time, my control would snap. . . ." He let the sentence hang in midair and swiped the towel across the tops of his shoes.

It took a minute for what he'd said to sink in, mostly because of the way he'd tossed it at her without verbal italics or exclamation marks. When it did, though, she took notice—bolting upright in the tub only to hit her head on the soap dish sticking out from the wall. Her fingers were trembling as she rubbed the resulting sore spot.

"Damn you, Tanner Flynn! How *dare* you imagine that I would put myself through that *wretched* experience all over again *just to get even*!" If her voice was a little too loud on that last bit, she could only blame it on the man staring at her with such compelling intensity.

His gaze drifted below her chin and stayed there. "I've never once thought of that night as wretched. Exciting, wondrous, and, yes, frustrating. But never wretched."

"It must have something to do with point of view," she said from between clenched teeth.

To her surprise he nodded, then wadded the towel into a loose ball and tossed it at her. It wasn't until she was hugging the thick terry cloth against her body that she realized she'd been sitting there totally exposed. When the telltale heat of an embarrassed flush didn't immediately appear, she was reminded of a similar lack of shyness or embarrassment the night she'd made love with Tanner.

"I'm glad to see some things don't change," he murmured thickly, and she thought his hand was less than steady as it dropped to the floor.

"What things?" she asked, her anger sidelined as she wondered if he was referring to her apparent lack of inhibitions. She'd come to the conclusion long ago that if she'd been the least bit hesitant, he might have realized sooner that she wasn't at all experienced.

"What things haven't changed?" she demanded when he didn't answer.

"Your breasts." He exhaled forcefully before he met her gaze. "They are every bit as pretty as I remember. Round and firm, and with nipples the color of a desert rose."

Her fingers dug into the towel as the blush she'd thought to be a nonplayer blossomed in her cheeks. "This is absurd, Tanner. Please get out of my bathroom."

He shook his head. "Not until you promise you're not doing this just to get even . . . because if you are, I won't do it."

"You won't do what?" She was getting confused.

"Make love to you."

"I haven't asked you to." Well, not yet anyway.

"But you're going to. I just wanted to warn you that if this is a little revenge scenario, it won't work."

Abby felt her jaw drop and wondered irrelevantly why a man whose expressions had been unfathomable for so long now looked conspicuously poker-faced—a classifiable distinction in her book. She glanced around for something to throw, and was contemplating the complimentary soap when he continued.

"A man can't be expected to go through that kind of torture twice in one lifetime."

"Making love to me was *torture*?" She figured the screech in her voice clued him in to the way she felt about that.

"Of course not. *Quitting* was torture. If we tried this again and you decided—for reasons that I'm sure you feel are warranted—to, er, stop things at a delicate moment, I seriously doubt I'd be able to accommodate you."

"What?"

He looked at her without blinking. "I wouldn't stop, Abby. I couldn't."

She could not believe what she was hearing, which was why, she supposed, she was able to reply. "You're acting as though last time it was my fault."

"It was."

"No it wasn't."

"It was."

"It wasn't!" she snapped, feeling like a schoolgirl having a fight with the class bully.

"It was." Tanner held up a hand to forestall her next volley. "If I'd had any idea you were a virgin, I wouldn't have come within ten miles of you. Now that you're not—"

She interrupted. "How do you know I'm not?"

"You said so."

"No, I didn't."

"Yes, you did," he said reasonably, but there was a slight edge to his words.

"I didn't."

"You did."

"Didn't."

"Did."

"I'm a virgin!" Her declaration swelled and echoed against the tiled walls in much the same way chamber music responds to excellent acoustics. There wasn't a doubt in Abby's mind that she was losing whatever sanity she had left. While shouting that little tidbit wasn't perhaps the best way to ensure Tanner's assistance, it did suffice to shut him up. He stared at her for the longest time, then seemed to relax where before he'd been slouched uncomfortably on the floor.

"You are?" he asked casually before scooting away from the tub to ease his back against the wall. He didn't seem in any hurry for an answer as he contemplated his fingernails, as though deciding whether or not they needed buffing.

"Yes." It was too late, she supposed, to wiggle her way out of giving that particular piece of information. Besides, he'd already confessed to changing his mind about that little barrier years ago. Not that she was one hundred percent certain that she believed him, but if he'd lied about changing his mind, she'd soon find out. Maybe. The way things were going, there was a good chance she'd kill him before they got that far.

"So, Abby, it appears that your breasts aren't the only things that haven't changed."

He looked so incredibly smug that the urge to hit him with something came over her again. She resisted —barely—sensing this might be her best chance to ensure there was no misunderstanding between them. "Yes, Tanner, I still am and always have been a virgin. If you can't handle that, then I suggest you get out of here before I scream for someone to throw you out."

"You've been screaming off and on for ten minutes,

and no one has interfered yet." He smiled affably. "I don't mind being yelled at so long as we're making progress."

It didn't escape her attention that he didn't get up and leave. A corner of the towel had fallen into the tub, and the thick fibers were currently absorbing the contents of her bath. It grew heavy and clammy against her skin, but she didn't even once consider letting go.

"The only progress being made here," she said, "is to demonstrate how stupid this plan was in the first place."

"At least you're admitting there is a plan."

"I'm admitting nothing." She took a deep, frustrated breath, a movement that caused the towel to dip precariously and allow a single nipple to pop over the edge. With an impatient "tsk," she pushed a soggy end up over the curve of her breast. She heard a curious groan from across the room.

"What's wrong?" she demanded, looking hard at him. She thought he looked a bit green around the gills, but decided it could be the lighting. "If you're going to be sick, go do it in your own room."

"I'm not sick."

"Go back to your room anyway. I'm getting cold in here, and I doubt if I can hold on to this towel much longer." She was also tired of trying to keep up with a dialogue that had long since crossed the line from logic to nonsense, but wasn't about to admit she couldn't hold her own.

"If you think I can walk in this condition, you're crazy." He groaned again and shut his eyes for a long moment. When he opened them to look at her, there was no mistaking the desire she saw in them. The movement of his hand pulled her gaze downward, and she watched spellbound as the tips of his long fingers traced the ridge of flesh at his crotch. His voice, when he spoke, was lower than before, rough and exciting like it had been that night in Aspen.

"Don't look so shocked, lass. This has been known to happen when all you've done is walk across a room."

She couldn't for the life of her think of anything to say. Neither could she tear her gaze from the swell of his erection.

"If that towel slips again," he went on, "I won't be responsible."

"For what?" She asked the question without thinking, then shuddered as he pushed the heel of his hand across the rigid flesh. He groaned again, and his hand fisted at his side.

"Don't ask stupid questions, Abby. I'm not in the mood." His words had an edge to them again, and she glanced up to see him scowling at her.

She said, "I do wish you'd make up your mind, Tanner. I can't decide whether you followed me to Rathmullan because you want to make love to me or because of a perverse desire to talk me to death."

"What I *want* is for you to come over here and kneel astride me so that when I unzip my jeans, I won't have to wait another second before I'm deep inside you." His chest heaved with each breath, and his fist thudded against the floor. "Unfortunately, your lack of experience prohibits me from asking you to do anything of the sort. While that position can serve to give the woman a certain amount of control, I doubt it would be the most comfortable way to lose your virginity."

Abby was about to make another suggestion that

involved what he could do with his smart-aleck come-
backs when there was a knock at the door.

With a groan that sounded remarkably like Tanner's, she stood up from the bath, careful to let the
towel fall across the parts of her that seemed to have a
paralyzing effect on Tanner.

He stared at her disbelievingly. "You're not going
to answer that, are you?"

"I have to," she whispered, then called out in a
louder voice, "I'll be right there." She climbed out of
the tub and paused beside it. "I told them to bring it
inside if I was out."

"What the hell was so important that you couldn't
wait for a more appropriate time?"

"Just a package I've been waiting for," she snapped.
"How was I supposed to know you'd be incapacitated
on my bathroom floor when they brought it?"

"I'm not incapacitated!"

"Then prove it by getting out of the way so I can
get to the door."

When he didn't budge, Abby lost her patience.
Leaving pools of water for footprints, she padded
across the floor to where he lay sprawled, and dumped
the sopping wet towel in his lap. Then, before his protest had progressed beyond words of one syllable, she'd
stepped across his legs, grabbed her robe from the
hook on the wall, and pulled it on.

Abby was signing the delivery receipt when she
heard movement behind her. She tensed, and was
strangely disappointed when the next identifiable
sound was that of the connecting door shutting.

It appeared that Tanner wasn't incapacitated after
all.

———◆———

He was, however, persistent.

Abby supposed she shouldn't have been surprised to come out of the bathroom after drying her hair and find Tanner, dry and clothed and ensconced in a deep chair near the bay windows. It was, after all, her own fault that she'd neglected to lock the connecting door after he'd fled through it. She just wished he didn't look so smug about it.

Tightening the sash of her floor-length crimson robe and pretending a nonchalance she didn't feel, Abby sauntered across the room to take the chair at the other end of the low coffee table.

"What's on your mind now, Tanner? If you've come to ferret out trade secrets, it won't do you any good. The package is in the bathroom, and I think you're too much of a gentleman to grab it while I'm looking." She tucked her legs under her bottom and carefully arranged the robe around her.

"Actually, I'm more interested in continuing our conversation." He touched his steepled fingertips to his chin and regarded her seriously. "I've waited a long time for you, Abby, but I never imagined that after three years, I would still be your first lover."

The way he just dove into the crux of things stole her breath. "I thought you didn't want to hear about other men."

"I don't, but still, I can't help but wonder. Why me?" He eased back in his chair, giving the impression he was only mildly interested in her answer. "It doesn't make sense, Abby, not with our history."

She'd had three years of practice avoiding his gaze,

and she did so now. "It has to do with closure, I suppose."

"What do you mean?"

Abby knew she had to tell him part of it, but instinctively kept part of it back. There was only so much of herself that she could afford to lose if it all went wrong. Taking a deep breath for courage, she looked up and deliberately met his gaze.

"Closure, Tanner, as in finish. The end." She blinked under his intent look, and tried to explain without giving him any loose ends to pull at. "In a way, it's like reading. I've never been able to read more than one book at a time, and I can't go on to another without finishing the one in hand—no matter how bad it is."

"You're comparing me to a bad book?"

She could see how he might get that impression, and the thought amused her. "Unfinished is all I was referring to," she said, "though I'm sorry I can't reassure you about the quality. To paraphrase your own verdict, my knowledge regarding the intimate goings-on between men and women is appallingly inaccurate."

He scowled. "What is it about you that makes me behave like an ass and talk like a fool? I never should have said anything of the sort to you."

"It's the truth, but never mind that now. We were talking about closure."

"Meaning you want to finish what we started."

"Yes. Maybe then I can get on with my life without feeling like I've left something undone," she added.

"That makes a certain kind of sense, I suppose."

"It's either that or throw the book away." Her shrug was part indecision, part indifference. "It took me three years to decide which would be more effective."

"I should feel relieved from my close call."

A decidedly uneasy feeling swept through Tanner when she said, "It was a lot closer than you imagine."

Looking at her, the way she held her head so proudly and met his gaze without flinching, he could believe it.

"Just one thing, though." He shrugged a single shoulder as though to ease a stretched muscle, but didn't let his gaze waver from her. "How will we know when it's over?"

"You mean *if* we decide to go through with this, don't you, Tanner? I don't know about you, but I'm not sure about anything."

"Just answer the question, Abby," he said smoothly. "The question of *if* anything happens is a whole other matter."

"How will we know when it's over?" A smile tugged at her lips. "Even with my limited experience, I would have thought that much was obvious."

It didn't take any effort at all to disagree with her, but he kept it simple because telling Abby he wanted a hell of a lot more than sex from her would raise issues he wasn't ready to address. Not rationally, anyway.

"A single orgasm isn't going to satisfy me," he said instead, "not when I've spent three years waiting for you. I'll want more from you than that, Abby. A lot more." He only felt a little guilty about the deep blush his blunt words had inflicted, and reconciled that, too, when he saw anger flare in her eyes.

"I'm inexperienced, Tanner, not stupid. You went without *me* for three years, not sex. There's a difference."

"You're sure about that, are you?"

"Of course I'm sure. And don't try to tell me you've been abstaining all this time because I won't buy it. If more than a week goes by without the society column running a photo of you with some woman on your arm, I know that you're either sick or out of town. One has to assume they were drooling over something besides the size of your wallet."

"Assumptions are dangerous things, Abby. You should be careful how you handle them." He should know. He'd made a big one about Abby, although he supposed that if he'd known her sex life was completely nonexistent, he doubted he could have waited as patiently . . . or as long.

It had been the assumption that there were other men in her life that had kept him from breaking his resolve to wait until she'd forgiven him—yes, *forgiven him*, because that was what it was all about. Knowing there must be other men had been his punishment, and he hadn't been able to do anything about it because until she took the first step, he had no rights.

"You're talking in riddles again," she said in a voice that was only slightly steadier than her fingers as she fiddled with the robe's deep-cut lapel. "I suppose I should apologize for razzing you about all the gorgeous women. It's none of my business why they choose to be with you. It's just that I assumed they were smart enough to realize there's more to you than a photo opportunity."

"You're still muddling up your assumptions." He figured she'd be stunned if she realized how far off base she was.

She scowled. "I haven't any idea what you mean."

He rested his forearms on his thighs and looked at

her carefully, wondering if now might be the time to tell her just how little any of those women meant to him. "It's sometimes hard to say things straight out. In our case, we haven't had much practice—"

It was her turn to interrupt as a look of stunned disbelief washed over her. "My God, Tanner, do you mean you're serious about Audrey or Andrea—"

"Angela is her name, and no, lass, I'm not serious about her or any of the others."

"I would never have invited you here if I'd known," she said as though he hadn't spoken.

"There's nothing to know."

She expelled a deep breath. "I've been so busy with my own agenda that I didn't even think you might be, well, involved. I mean *seriously*. It's just that you change them—women, I mean—so often—"

He interrupted again. "Stop it, Abby. I want to talk about the women in my life even less than I want to hear about the men in yours."

She looked at him for what seemed a very long time. "Then what *do* you want to talk about?"

He thought about what he'd almost told her, then decided it was better left for another time. At the moment, she looked like she'd had enough for one day. He stood and pulled her up from her chair, not stopping until she was standing toe-to-toe with him. "Let's give it a rest for now, Abby. We can get back to true confessions another time."

"It's nice to know I've got something easy to look forward to," she said smoothly.

"Why's that?"

"*I've* got nothing to confess."

FOUR

Abby's indecision didn't lessen Tanner's desire for her at all, and necessity compelled him to strip down and endure a freezing shower before changing for dinner. His skin was still on the chilled side as he got into the tie and dinner jacket that he assumed was required costume for dinner amidst all the sparkling crystal and gleaming silver he'd glimpsed during his earlier recon of the facilities. By the time he stooped in front of the too-low dresser mirror to adjust the knot of his tie, he was reasonably confident that he'd be able to get through the night without succumbing to his need to drag Abby behind a closed door and make hard, fast love to her.

Thanks to the shower, he was in too much control to allow something he'd looked forward to for so long be finished that quickly. More important, though, was that of the thousand times he'd made love to her in his dreams, the one that made him the craziest was when he took her soft and slow, drawing out their pleasure until their bodies were slickened with sweat and her moans of pleasure became cries of unbearable need.

The image of Abby, naked and open to his every whim, brought a groan of near-pain from deep inside. Blood pooled in his groin, but he was determined to ignore the heavy throbbing as he straightened and grabbed a strip of leather from the dresser. His fingers were on the clumsy side as he tied back his hair and flicked a bit of lint from the lapel of his charcoal-colored jacket. His knuckles lingered for a moment on the soft cashmere, and he wondered how long it would be before he was able to test Abby's sensitivity to different textures.

It was just one of many things they hadn't gotten to that night in Aspen.

With a sigh of anticipation-laced frustration, he buttoned his jacket over the bulge of his erection and strode from the room. Thinking a drink would ease the tension, he made quick work of the two flights of stairs that led to the cellar bar.

He couldn't decide whether to be pleased or miffed to discover Abby had beaten him to it. Wrapped in a rose-colored silk number that showed off her spectacular legs and accented her soft curves in modest detail, she sat alone by the fire with a cordial glass in one hand. It occurred to Tanner that he'd rarely seen her sitting by herself; Abby was a gregarious creature by nature and made friends faster than bunnies made bunnies. Drawing closer, he noticed something in her expression that jerked him from his erotic preoccupation and filled him with an uneasy sense of forboding. He got a drink from the bar and went over to join her on a padded bench.

She didn't look up until his thigh brushed hers as

he settled beside her, but not even that small gesture of familiarity managed to smooth the worry from her brow. She didn't scoot away, though, just looked at him with her eyebrows slanted in puzzlement and her bottom lip caught between her teeth.

Tanner took a sip of the single malt Irish whiskey and waited for her to tell him what the problem was so he could fix it. After several longish minutes during which the crackling of the fire was the only sound, he realized that she was looking straight through him.

He decided he didn't want to wait after all. "What's happened, lass?"

She looked into the fire, her fingers laced around the small stemmed glass. "Sandra backed out of the deal. I just got a fax from my office a few minutes ago."

He could see why she was upset, and resolved to get the whole story out of her, thinking that sharing her worries would ease them. "Any idea why?"

She started to shake her head, then hesitated. "My accountant just said she appeared to change her mind, but . . ."

"You think there's something more to it?" he asked when she didn't finish her thought.

Another minute hesitation, then she looked up at him. "I'm worried that someone helped her change her mind."

It was Tanner's turn to hesitate. If Abby knew enough to suspect someone of sabotaging her deal with Sandra, then this wasn't the first time she'd been confronted with a problem of this nature.

The notion that her decision to sell might be based on something other than a desire to move on chilled him more thoroughly than the cold shower had. "Has someone been threatening you, Abby?"

"Threats are only useful if you believe them. In this case, I've got no reason to think they're anything more than empty words." The ghost of a smile touched her lips. "I'm a big girl, Tanner. There isn't anything here for you to be concerned with."

"Like hell there isn't," he growled. "If someone is harassing you, then it's very much my business." Slaying her dragons was his job, his *right*. He hadn't watched over her for three years to stand idly on the sidelines while she did battle.

She patted his hand as one might soothe a puppy eager to fight the overgrown bulldog in the next garden. "Excuse me for a minute, will you? I've got a call to make."

Tanner got to his feet with the intention of going with her, but she moved too fast. Abby was through the bar and out the door before he'd gotten five feet.

"So much for being needed," he muttered aloud. Downing his drink, he went over to the bar and got into a discussion with the man on the next stool about the merits of Irish whiskey versus Scotch. They were just getting into a somewhat friendly debate over the rumored Irish origins of a certain premium Japanese whiskey when Abby returned. Tanner bid a quick good-bye to the man and followed her back to the fire.

She stood with her hands stretched toward the flames and spoke to him over her shoulder. "I called Sandra. She confirmed what I suspected."

"She's been forced to withdraw?" At her nod, he asked, "How?"

"She didn't say exactly, just that he made it clear she'd be healthier if she stayed in the restaurant business."

"Who's *he*?"

"Again, she didn't say."

"But you think it was Yoshimoto, don't you?"

Surprise flickered in her eyes. "What makes you say that?"

"Just putting two and two together. You mentioned at Grianan of Aileach that he was being persistent. It fits."

She turned away without verifying his guess, but she hadn't denied it either, so he assumed he was tracking along the same path as Abby was. Resting an elbow on the mantel over the fire, he looked down at her.

"Come on, Abby, what's going on here?"

It occurred to Abby that he was using the same tone of voice as he'd used when she'd told him about Samuels. It bothered her—not that Tanner was concerned, but that he would feel the need to interfere in what was essentially a business matter. She decided she wasn't going to allow that.

Yoshimoto was her problem.

"I can handle this, Tanner. I'm sorry now that I said anything about it." She lowered her gaze, then found herself looking into his eyes as he forced her chin upward with the gentle but insistent pressure of his hand.

"Sandra Harringdon isn't the kind of woman to buckle under pressure—not unless she judged the risk not worth the prize. For her to give up something she wants, the risk must have been substantial. The fact that you suspected something before you even spoke to her indicates there's a lot more going on here than you're telling me." His eyes glinted behind partially lowered lashes, making him look as dangerous as he sounded. Then he quietly added, "I can't be your lover and ignore anything that affects you—no matter how much you want me to."

Her heart thudded at his almost casual presumption of their relationship. "You're not my lover, not yet, maybe not ever."

"Don't complicate this with semantics, Abby. We've been lovers in one way or another ever since that night in Aspen. Just because you've been pretending otherwise won't change things."

"We're not—" She fell silent beneath his glare.

"Lovers tease and flirt and fight, just like we've been doing all these years. Lovers can't be in the same room without knowing exactly where the other is standing, just as they can't keep from looking at each other—even if they then pretend they weren't looking at all. *Lovers*—" he said just a touch louder when she opened her mouth to interrupt, "go to sleep thinking of each other and wake up the same way."

A small group of people came into the bar, causing Tanner to turn his back so that she was shielded from their curious stares. She blinked back her confusion at his intensity and said, "And here I thought lovers were people who . . . well, made love."

"Only in an ideal world," he murmured, his gaze taking in the growing color in her face as his fingers delved into the silky curls behind her ears. "What I was getting at, though, was the part of their relationship where they look after each other. That's all I'm trying to do, Abby. Look after you."

"And what if I decide against making love with you?"

His expression reverted to something unreadable. "It's your decision, Abby. Let's hope it's the right one for both of us."

"You've already made yours?" she asked, then continued without waiting for his answer. "I thought you were still weighing the risks."

"That was bravado, lass, nothing more. I wouldn't be here now if I didn't know what I wanted." His gaze narrowed on hers. "I won't say no to you, but I won't make up your mind for you either. None of this changes what I said before, though. I still want to look after you."

There was a lump in her throat that made it difficult to speak. "All the same, Tanner, this is one time when I'm perfectly capable of looking after myself."

The implacable tone in her voice warned Tanner against pushing any harder . . . for the moment. In any case, there were other ways of handling things. If he couldn't get rid of the problem, then he could take steps to ensure her stubbornness didn't expose her to harm. He'd protect her whether she liked it or not.

As for making love, he knew he'd go along with whatever she decided. Despite all the teasing and prodding he'd put her through that afternoon, he would never go against what she wanted, no matter what price he ended up paying.

He already loved her. Whether or not they made love would have no bearing on how he'd feel if he lost her. Either way, his heart wouldn't be worth a penny valentine.

Smoothing his hand across her shoulder, he forced a smile. "Your pigheadedness was the second thing that attracted me to you."

"What was the first?" she asked, not seeming to mind what other women might have interpreted as a slur on their character.

He just shook his head and suggested they go into dinner. It wasn't, he decided, in his best interest to admit he'd admired her aggressive business demeanor long before he'd noticed she was a woman.

Her being short, blond, and perky had kept him blind right up until that night when she'd sashayed into the Aspen hotel and laughed her way into his heart.

Dinner was a subdued affair during which Abby nibbled at the excellent fare in a distracted silence and Tanner watched her do it. He attempted, at first, to tease her into a lighter mood, then tried talking about her new business venture when that didn't work. In the end, he gave her what he realized she wanted most: Undemanding companionship.

Neither ordered a sweet course, and when it came time to go into the adjoining room for coffee, Abby said she would take hers up to her room. Tanner declined a cup, waited as she poured one for herself, then followed her up the elegantly railed staircase. The moment they arrived at her door and she turned with what he assumed was a polite good night on her lips, Tanner reached beyond her to turn the knob and push open the door. Before she could object, he'd edged past her to enter the room. He was drawing closed the heavy drapes when she caught up with him.

"What do you think you're doing, Tanner?"

Putting my mind at ease, he said to himself. While Abby might disregard the threats—whatever they might entail—he was incapable of following her example. Until she decided to share her worries, her trust, he would have to take care of her without appearing to. That included making sure someone hadn't entered her unlocked room in her absence.

"If you're thinking about staying—"

He interrupted without raising his voice. "I wouldn't dream of it, Abby. You're not in the mood, and I'm too jet-lagged to mind." Tanner could have sworn he heard a disgruntled noise that could only have come from her, but he decided it was best not to query it. If she denied "not being in the mood," he'd be left with the decision between her and jet lag. The mere fact that he realized there was a decision meant he was too tired to give her the attention she deserved.

He would do it, though, if she insisted.

Just to be on the safe side, he decided not to give her even a hint that he was anything more than totally exhausted. Assuming a bland expression, he went over to turn down her bed. "Don't mind me, Abby. I've always fancied myself as a ladies' maid." He ignored her skeptical expression as he made a show of fluffing her pillows. "There should be another of these in the closet. Shall I check?"

"Don't both—"

He spun and opened the closet before she could finish. Grabbing a pillow from the top shelf of the uninhabited cubicle, he tossed it onto the bed, then knelt down for a quick peek under it. He straightened and put a peevish note in his voice when he asked, "Where are your slippers? I can't find them."

She groaned and flopped into one of the soft-cushioned chairs, her blond curls splayed against the burgundy velvet. "Go away, Tanner. Whatever you're looking for, I don't have any."

He agreed. No one was hiding in this room, not now anyway. Rising from his knees, he tried to look chagrined, but gave it up when he realized she'd shut her eyes. He was glad, because lying to her was easier when she wasn't looking.

"I was hoping for a glimpse of that package you got this afternoon," he said.

She grinned without opening her eyes. "I gave it to the manager for safekeeping."

"You wound me." He clutched his heart for dramatic effect as her eyes fluttered open. "How dare you imagine I'd stoop so low?"

"You've stooped much lower than searching my room," she reminded him as she reached for her coffee. "As I recall, you not only searched my room last year in Hong Kong, but you also stole the sample book I'd borrowed from that silk factory."

He rounded the bed and grinned down at her. "I simply wanted to return the book to its rightful owners."

"And ace me out of the fabrics I'd chosen for some very special blouses." The cup should have cracked when she slammed it back onto its saucer, but it didn't. Tanner imagined it was because the cup, like Abby, was stronger than it looked.

He hadn't searched her room because he underestimated her; Abby could, in most circumstances, take care of herself. He'd done it so he could get a good night's rest. With jet lag tearing at his nerves, he'd sleep easier if he didn't have to do it with his ear to the wall.

"We made a lot of money on the dresses we got from that silk," he said, "but I can see you're not going to make things easy for me tonight."

"What makes you think I'm doing any shopping at all this trip?"

He gave a short laugh. "I know you too well, Abby. If you're not juggling three balls in one hand and balancing a tray of martinis in the other, you're either sick or ready to move on to the next target. You *never* just do one thing at a time."

"I don't like martinis."

"That's not the point. I don't believe for one second that you plan to go home empty-handed from Ireland. It would be out of character for you to come all this way just for personal reasons. That's not enough to keep you busy."

He was kind of glad she didn't respond to that, because he knew he could keep her very, very busy if she would only say the word . . . which she hadn't, not yet. "Think you can rouse yourself enough to lock the door behind me?"

Her eyebrows danced wickedly. "*Doors*, you mean. I seem to remember you pointing out there are two to this room."

"Doors," he agreed reluctantly. Still, he thought that the way she sat, slouched deep into the chair, proved her trust of him went deeper than he'd ever imagined.

She couldn't have known how much she tempted him with her laughing eyes and sweet curves that he remembered being as smooth as the finest silk. She couldn't have known, because if she did, she wouldn't be sitting there with her legs sprawled inelegantly in front of her and her dress creeping up her thighs.

She couldn't have known, because if she did, then she wasn't the kind, warmhearted woman he glimpsed between bouts of pigheaded orneriness.

"Go away, Tanner," she said, her voice a husky drawl. "I promise I don't have any shopping scheduled for tomorrow. We can both sleep in."

A frustrated groan caught in his throat, but before she could ask what was wrong, he said good night and left the room via the connecting door. Shutting it behind him, he turned the key—just in case Abby decided to attack him in the middle of the night—then put his ear to the door in time to hear the silver bells of her laughter.

Tanner kept his ear right where it was until he was satisfied that she'd locked both doors, then he strode past the bed to the phone. Tugging at the knot of his tie with one hand, he pulled a small book from his breast pocket with the other and dialed his assistant. If there was anything to be learned about Yoshimoto in Phoenix, Tanner was confident Cummings would discover it.

Twenty minutes later, he'd finished a second call to a man in Singapore about the same subject and was debating on whether to make a third call when he remembered Abby had only promised she wasn't going shopping the next day. She hadn't said anything about hanging around the hotel until he roused from what he expected to be a long sleep.

Sighing, he picked up the phone and dialed his cousin's number in Northern Ireland. Tanner spent the few seconds before the connection was made wondering if he was destined to spend the rest of his life trying to keep two steps ahead of the woman he loved.

FIVE

It was still dark when Tanner was summoned from sleep by a soft knock on his door. The luminous dial on the bedside clock said it was just gone seven, and the only way he was able to drag his body from the bed was with a promise that he'd be back between the sheets before he'd fully awakened.

On the off chance that it wasn't who he was expecting, he grabbed his robe from the hook in the bathroom and pulled it on. He was fumbling with the belt when the knock sounded again and the muted whisper of his name floated through the wood.

Pausing just long enough to throw open the dead bolt, he went into the bathroom and left his early-morning caller to let himself into the room. By the time he'd splashed enough water on his face to attain a reasonable level of alertness, his guest had made himself comfortable in the sitting area beyond the bed and was pouring coffee from a thermos. An expensive-looking leather car coat fit snugly across the man's broad shoulders, and the slacks and sweater he wore looked equally appropriate for a country hotel where a single night's stay could feed a family of four for a week.

Tanner eased his exhausted body into the chair opposite and looked through bleary eyes at his cousin, thinking that even his short and conservative haircut looked expensive—an amazing change from the shaggy-dog look he'd been sporting just a few months past.

"Any trouble getting in?" he asked.

Rory O'Neill shook his head. "I laid low in my car until the day staff began to arrive, then told the manager I'd been driving all night—which wasn't far from the truth. My room is at the other end of the hall. Want some coffee?"

"Yes, but I won't. Now that you're here, I can get some real sleep." He ignored the tantalizing aroma hanging in the air and yawned twice. His ears were still popping when he realized Rory was speaking. "Say again?"

Rory paused midsentence, then shook his head and started over. "Did something in particular happen to make you call me, or are you operating on instinct?"

"Instinct. That and a rumor I heard a few months ago in Phoenix about Yoshimoto." Tanner remembered how Abby had skated around the question of why she didn't want to sell to Yoshimoto, and wondered if she'd heard the same rumor. "The computer company he bought into in Phoenix had been privately held by two brothers named Marshall and was a healthy concern before Yoshimoto added his name to the letterhead. There was a suspicion he somehow forced his way in."

"Any chance of talking to either of the brothers?"

"I've got my assistant working on that. Since it's

Sunday, it might be as late as tomorrow evening before we hear anything."

Rory refilled his cup. "In the meantime, give me what background you can. If I'm hiring on as minder, I need to know everything you do." Minder was the Anglo-Irish term for bodyguard, and the reason Tanner had sent for Rory. He not only wanted Abby watched, he wanted her protected.

Tanner pressed his steepled fingers to the bridge of his nose and tried to remember what he'd already told his cousin. It had been the third call he'd made the night before, one that made sense because Abby, being Abby, was a handful in normal circumstances. Now that it seemed her life was getting a tad complicated, Tanner had decided professional help was essential. His cousin—ex-SAS and now a freelance troubleshooter (for lack of a better description)—fitted his needs precisely. With Rory's help, he could keep Abby out of whatever trouble lurked, be it imagined or real.

He wasn't about to wait for something bad to happen to be convinced there was a threat.

Tanner gave Rory the few details he'd gleaned from Abby about the sale of Desert Reef, filling in the gaps with sketchy backgrounds on both Sandra Harringdon and Kenji Yoshimoto. Then he told Rory about Abby herself and why it might be a touch difficult to keep track of her. Rory was openly skeptical of one small woman's ability to bedevil a grown man, so Tanner ended up telling his cousin about the time in Sicily when she'd eluded him on the way to the villa. And about how she'd stranded him in Singapore. By the time he finished his recitation with the tale of how Abby had managed to dislodge a plaid-shirted masher in an Alaskan bar without any noticeable effort, Rory looked considerably more respectful of Tanner's blond nemesis—if not, perhaps, of Tanner himself.

"So you think the two of us are big enough to keep her out of harm's way?" Rory asked, screwing the lid back onto his thermos. "You make it sound as though a whole platoon might be needed to keep up with her."

"A whole platoon would be helpful, but wouldn't blend into the scenery. You will." He dragged a hand through his hair and tried valiantly to keep his eyes open. "Abby is determined that she can handle whatever is going on. I'd rather she doesn't know about you."

"Afraid she'll be upset with you for taking over?"

Tanner laughed. "I'm more concerned that she'll give you the slip if she finds out you're following her. I know you're good, but she's tricky."

"What she sounds is dangerous," Rory said. "Can't you convince her Yoshimoto is bad news?"

"Not until I have proof. Right now, it's just a feeling made stronger by her disinclination to talk about it."

"What if she decides not to tell you anything at all?"

"Given that streak of independence of hers, I thought it best not to wait. Besides the Marshall brothers, I called a man I know who lives in Singapore—"

Rory interrupted. "This wouldn't be someone you met when you were stranded there, would it?"

Tanner grinned. "Abby never knew what a favor she did me back then. I ended up staying in a hotel belonging to Wyatt Conners, one of the big wheels in the Pacific Rim. Most of the tourists and such had sensibly gotten out before the typhoon hit, so those of us who stayed got to know each other rather well." He paused for a moment, remembering the marathon poker game and how Wyatt had felt so bad about taking him to the cleaners, he'd offered Tanner a previously unexploited contact for inexpensive Asian merchandise. Tanner had ended up making a small fortune on that deal and the subsequent ones that Wyatt had channeled in his direction.

If Abby had actually bought the Spanish triptyches, he might have felt free to gloat. But she hadn't, and the last thing he needed was for Abby to perceive a win on his side of the scoreboard. She was too good at getting even.

Rory's polite "ahem" pulled Tanner from his mental meanderings. He opened his eyes and wondered when they'd shut. "I think I was about to tell you that I called Wyatt last night and asked him to check out Yoshimoto. If he's got as much money as he's been throwing around Phoenix, someone out on the Rim should have heard of him."

Rory stood to leave. "You get some rest. So long as you've got her keys, all I've got to worry about is the front door. I'll be able to cover that from the lounge. They keep a pot of coffee going in there, so I won't appear to be lurking. I don't suppose you know if she's the only five foot blond, gray-eyed woman staying here?"

Tanner picked up his wallet from the table between them and took out a photograph that was worn with age. For the first time since Rory had knocked, he made an effort to fully focus his eyes, and was rewarded by the familiar sight of Abby's laughing profile. He'd discovered the photo two years earlier on a bulletin board filled with candid shots of convention attendees, and had appropriated it without a single misgiving. He handed it to Rory, who looked at it carefully before giving it back.

"Don't worry, Tanner. I'll take care of your woman."

"If she was really mine, she'd share her troubles and you wouldn't be forced to skulk in the shadows."

"Just because she doesn't know it doesn't mean she isn't yours." Rory went to the door and left without hardly making a sound.

Tanner's last thought before falling asleep again was that he'd forgotten to warn Rory about Abby's overly friendly nature. He didn't let it worry him, though.

Rory knew better than to let a subject get too close.

Tantalizing aromas of whatever was being served for lunch pestered Tanner's growing appetite, and it took considerable willpower not to head straight for the dining room where he assumed Abby was already enjoying a wonderful meal. Before he joined her, though, he figured he'd better let Rory know he was on duty. He didn't want his cousin floating away on a river of coffee. The additional five hours of sleep that had left Tanner feeling contented and much more in control of things had likely bored his cousin into a mild stupor.

Taking a left at the bottom of the staircase, he went into the spacious sitting room and wound his way between heavily cushioned chairs to the bay window where Rory was sitting. Something in his cousin's mildly panicked expression made Tanner hesitate before speaking . . . which was a good thing, because a familiar feminine voice stepped into the breach and jerked his sense of well-being right out from under him.

"I would have thought that a man who travels as much as you do would know better than to let jet lag bully him into sleeping so late."

Tanner felt the blood leave his face as he looked aside to discover Abby ensconced in a high-backed wing chair that had hidden her from view. Dressed casually in matching powder-blue slacks and a bulky cable-knit sweater, she looked warm and cozy and full of mischief. His mind reeled with possible reasons that would explain why she was sitting opposite a man she wasn't supposed to notice, much less know well enough to share a pot of coffee with—which, from the evidence on the tea tray, was precisely what they'd been doing.

Abby shook her head and sighed dramatically. "Honestly, Tanner, if you're not awake enough to even say 'good morning,' you might as well go back to bed and sleep until tomorrow. You look like you need it."

Somehow, that didn't surprise him. "Good morning," he said automatically, then was stumped for anything else to say once he'd ruled out, "Sorry, I didn't notice you hiding in that chair." She'd want to know then why he'd approached Rory, and Tanner was momentarily short of explanations.

"Perhaps a cup of coffee would help loosen your tongue," she suggested, and took a sip from her own cup.

With her back momentarily turned to him, Tanner mouthed "How?" to Rory. Rory just lifted one shoulder in an almost unnoticeable shrug without changing the expression on his face. Not knowing what else to do, Tanner grabbed at the momentary reprieve Abby had offered and went over to the mahogany sideboard where he served himself from the large silver pot. He took his time, fiddling with sugar and cream—although he didn't normally use either—and was thinking how much simpler everything would be if she'd only trusted him enough to share her troubles.

Finding Rory and Abby together was a serious complication to his plan of keeping his cousin incognito, although he supposed he had only himself to blame for not warning Rory earlier. The dilemma that faced him now was discovering how much she knew without giving anything away, if there was anything left to give. If Abby had noticed Rory's early-morning visit to his room, Tanner wouldn't be doing himself any favors by pretending not to know him. If, on the other hand, Tanner admitted knowing him, he wouldn't have any idea what Rory had told her about himself.

All he could do was hope Rory was better at this guessing-game business than he was. Going back to stand beside Abby's chair, he smiled down at her and prayed Rory would dive in and tell him what the hell was going on before it was too late. "I trust you slept well, Abby?"

It was Abby herself—bless her heart—who saved him. "Very well, Tanner, but never mind. My manners appear to be as slow to surface as yours. We've been ignoring Mr. O'Neill. He's from Northern Ireland, and has been telling me all about the beautiful coastal area where he lives. I think he's convinced me that I need to see it before I leave Ireland." She proceeded to make the introductions with an ease that comforted Tanner because it was so wonderfully clear that she didn't have the faintest idea Rory and he were already acquainted.

On cue, Rory stood and offered his hand, humor

lighting his eyes within an otherwise controlled expression as they exchanged polite greetings. Since their meeting early that morning, Rory had transformed himself into something that was a cross between country squire and city suit weekending in the country with a tweed jacket and paisley ascot. Tanner thought the pipe poking out of his breast pocket was a nice touch.

"Are you in Rathmullan on business or pleasure?" Tanner asked, hoping it was the correct amount of curiosity.

Rory grinned. "A wee bit of both. I've got a cousin who I don't see much of, and as I was coming this way, I thought I'd look him up." Rory's accent was thicker than Tanner had ever heard it, a far cry from the faint lilt he normally spoke with. Tanner was scrambling for an appropriately polite response when Abby intervened.

"If you two don't sit down, I'll get a crick in my neck." With a familiar touch on his arm, she nudged Tanner into the chair she'd abandoned and perched on the corner of the coffee table as Rory sank back into his seat.

"Your, er, cousin lives near here?" Tanner asked.

"For the moment," Rory replied blithely, then glanced at Abby. "Miss Roberts was just telling me about your visit to Grianan of Aileach yesterday. Being Irish yourself, you must be aware the fort was held by the Clan O'Neill for almost seven centuries?"

"I'm afraid my knowledge of Irish history went the same path as my accent," Tanner admitted, groaning inwardly as Rory scored a point in their long-running argument over whether Tanner had gained more than he'd lost by emigrating with his father to the States so many years ago.

"'Tis a shame, that," Rory said, his smile offering consolation. "Perhaps if you stay long enough, it'll come back to you. Now if you'll excuse me, I must make a call."

"You're not joining us for lunch?" Abby asked.

Tanner added his vote, hoping to make Rory squirm for that last crack. Maybe if he had to keep up this pantomime for another hour or so, Rory would think twice before taking any more cheap shots. "Yes, Mr. O'Neill. Abby and I would enjoy hearing more about your home."

Rory was on top of things, though, and managed to slip away almost before Tanner finished speaking. Tanner stood and watched him go, then glanced down at Abby who had risen beside him. "You're looking more chipper this morning. Any particular reason?"

"Nothing that I want to spend lunch talking about. Let's just say I've finally found a way to convince Yoshimoto that I won't be bullied. By the time he realizes it's a ruse, Sandra will be the new owner of the boutique."

Fear welled inside him, and he couldn't help it that his grip on her arm was less than gentle as he pulled her around to face him. "What have you done, Abby?"

Her eyes widened in reaction to his intensity. "Nothing that you wouldn't have done, Tanner, if you were in the same position."

"That's not an answer."

"It's the only one you're going to get. I thought you understood last night that I could take care of this without your . . . help." During her meaningful hesitation, the word "interference" screamed silently between them. Her expression was hard and determined, her eyes flashing in the closest thing he'd ever seen to anger in her. He'd seen her annoyed, irritated, but never angry. "This has nothing to do with you, Tanner. Try to remember that."

"And *you* try to remember that not everyone plays fair," he ground out, trying desperately to hang on to his own temper. "Some people conduct business without paying attention to the rules."

"So far, all Yoshimoto has done is threaten," she returned furiously, "which is a far sight less than what Samuels did for you in Scotland. It's only thanks to luck and a good dog that I'm here at all!"

Tanner flipped gears at Abby's reference to Samuels. Whatever the man had done was serious enough that it had blinded her to what she considered to be mere threats from Yoshimoto. Since he couldn't very well beat the information out of Samuels—which he would have done if the man were anywhere nearby—Tanner decided he'd have to get it out of Abby.

He'd use a gentle touch, but he'd get it out of her all the same.

"We can't talk about this here. Come upstairs and you can tell me all about Samuels."

"You mean so you can yell at me."

"Exactly," he said through clenched teeth. "We already know we can get away with it up there."

"After lunch—"

"*Now!*" Without further argument, he turned her away from the dining room and headed toward the stairs. When she tried to pull away, he slid an arm around her waist, then bent down to stifle her protests by closing his mouth firmly over hers. He felt the shock go straight through her, and knew it was the audacity of his kiss rather than any physical response to it that sucked the fight out of her.

It took less than a second and lasted a lifetime. Her lips were as soft and sweet as he remembered, and he couldn't help the impulse that drove him to steal another kiss, quickly, before she came up with a reason that he shouldn't. When he lifted his head and looked into her upturned face, she was staring at him with a look of such bewilderment that he nearly laughed. The anger roiling inside of him was soothed by her innocent confusion, making him wonder how one woman could send him yo-yoing between emotional extremes without causing him to resent her hold on the string.

"What are you confused about, lass? The kiss or the reason for it?"

"Both," she murmured, then looked self-consciously aside. "Don't you feel a little conspicuous doing that in public?"

"It seemed the easiest way to win the argument you were determined to have." He did laugh then, at her attempt to organize an affronted expression on her face, then he coaxed her with a gentle tug to his side as he resumed his march out of the room. "As for the other part, to anyone watching—although you know as well as I do that no one would admit to any such thing —it was no more than a properly affectionate kiss. There was a couple in the lounge last night doing a lot more, and no one paid them any attention."

"So it was nothing." She sounded just a touch put out, and he pulled her tighter against him as they slowly mounted the stairs.

"It was the first time I've kissed you in three years, Abby, so I'd say it was a lot more than nothing." They got to her door and he opened it without letting go of her. Once inside, he backed her against the nearest wall and held her there with the warm pressure of his body as his hands flattened on the wall on either side of her face. "Now I want to kiss you like I couldn't downstairs."

As Tanner bent to nuzzle the soft skin under her ear, Abby heard herself whimper. It had been so long since she'd felt this way, three years since her body had trembled in response to Tanner's caress. Now, with his body warm and hard against hers, there was an excitement building in her that she'd never come close to feeling with any other man.

No other man had been able to make her want him. None had even come close.

Her hands lifted almost of their own accord to stroke the broad, familiar expanse of his shoulders. The cashmere sweater he wore was like furry satin beneath her palms, and she couldn't resist burying her fingers in the luxurious knit. Beneath the sweater and his cotton shirt, his shoulders flexed hard and tense, almost as if he were lifting weights even though there was no more than the weight of her face in his hands.

"I thought you brought me up here to yell at me," she murmured, digging her nails into his shoulders as his tongue traced the outer shell of her ear.

"I'll get to that." His lips skated across her cheek to the bridge of her nose, then down the other side. "Right now, the only sounds I want to hear are those sweet moans you make when I do something you like."

"By making love to me?"

"No, Abby. Just kissing. I'm too weak from hunger to do anything more." He brushed his mouth across hers, then did it again and smiled when she tried to follow his mouth with her lips. "Besides, I wasn't aware you'd made up your mind on that issue yet."

"I haven't." The pink tip of her tongue swept between her lips, and she lifted on her toes to take her own turn at teasing his mouth. Between quick, soft kisses, she said, "I was just thinking that if you put your mind to it and kept your mouth shut, there wouldn't be any decisions to make."

"You'd hate it if I kept my mouth shut." To prove the point, Tanner parted his lips over hers and began to make slow, wet love to her mouth. His tongue rasped across hers, then withdrew to thrust again and again, one hand threading into the curls at her nape to tilt her face higher as the other slid around her waist and lifted her hard against his body.

Abby didn't notice that her feet had left the floor, didn't care that she could hardly breathe in his tight embrace. Other things were important, things like how his long, thick hair felt like silk between her fingers, and how the heat between her legs grew with every thrust of his tongue. Even with layers of clothing between them, the hard strength of his erection was an unmistakable imprint against her belly.

His hand slid down to cup her bottom, and in response she wrapped one leg around his thigh. Tanner rocked against her, using the wall for balance as his mouth made heated love to hers.

Sanity was an unwelcome intrusion, first glimpsed when Tanner realized he was gripping her thigh as he tried to ease the hardness in his groin against her softness. It surfaced again with greater insistence moments later when he felt her fingers tugging at the top button of his shirt.

With a groan of genuine regret, he let her slide down his body until her hips were once again well below the level of his own and her mouth was a good six inches away. His thumb stroked her cheekbone until her eyes finally fluttered open. The gray orbs were filled with the smoky residue of fireworks, and her mouth was swollen and dewy from their mating.

She looked as ready to make love as any woman he'd ever had, and Tanner knew that he'd rather walk over hot coals than stop.

Unfortunately, sanity had intruded for a reason. He dropped his forehead to meet hers and said, "We should probably move on to the yelling part before I forget I promised this was your decision."

"What if I tell you I've decided to make love with you?"

A gut kick would have been kinder than Abby's tremulous response; pain easier to ignore than her offer of heaven. He did it, though, because somewhere at the periphery of his thoughts was the knowledge that she hadn't yet realized the stakes.

Tanner was in this for keeps, not just to fulfill some unfinished fantasy. If he had any chance at all of making it work, then he had to share her life, not just her body. A beginning was all he asked, and he'd settle for Samuels. Yoshimoto, he figured, would come later.

He let out a long breath and lifted his head a couple of inches. "Tell me that again when you've examined the consequences and know you can live with them."

"What consequences?"

"Us." It took an effort, but he eased his body away from hers and turned to walk to the windows. Staring blankly out over the mist-shrouded gardens, he said, "You asked me to Ireland to finish something between us. I came because I wanted a chance at having what I passed up three years ago."

"I still don't see the consequences. It all seems pretty straightforward to me." Her voice came from

somewhere nearby, yet he knew without looking that
she wasn't close enough to touch. She'd learned caution, he realized, and wished he hadn't been the one to
teach her.

"I didn't know until I saw you at Grianan of Aileach
that I was willing to risk it all for you." He turned and
found her standing near the foot of the bed, the color
missing from her face and her hands fisted in the bulky
sweater at her thighs. "If you let me close to you again,
I'm very much afraid you'll have trouble getting rid of
me when you're ready to go your own way. I won't
leave you willingly, Abby, and I'll fight to keep you
from leaving me."

A sharp intake of breath was her only response, and
Tanner had to force himself to remain silent as she
sorted through his words. He'd said enough, he knew.
Anything more would be superfluous. With his heart
pounding in his chest, he waited and wished he'd had
the sense to take what she offered without making
things so damned complicated.

It shouldn't matter that he wanted her forever, but
it did.

When she spoke, her voice was surprisingly steady.
"You're right about those consequences, Tanner. It
sounds as though I should probably think about them."

It was only with a tremendous effort that he kept
his disappointment from showing. "Let's go take a
walk, Abby. The bedroom was a lousy idea."

"What about lunch?"

"We'll get something in town." He went to the
connecting door that he'd unlocked from his side earlier and flipped open the bolt. "Get your coat, Abby,"
he said as he went to do the same. When he came back,

she was shrugging into the navy pea coat that made her seem smaller, more fragile than he knew her to be.

Her chin took on a stubborn tilt. "I'm not going to talk about business, no matter how much you yell."

"You'll tell me about Samuels, or I'll give you something to yell about," he promised, and snagged her hand to lead her out into the hall. "As for the other thing, you're playing with fire, Abby. Yoshimoto isn't going to go away without a fight."

"How do you know that?"

He paused at the top of the stairs and caught her chin in his palm. "The same way you know I'm serious about us. Instinct."

SIX

They ended up getting some sandwiches from the kitchen on their way outdoors, a detour Abby insisted upon when Tanner's stomach growled not once, but twice before they'd reached the bottom of the stairs. The kitchen staff must have been used to preparing take-away food with no notice, because they produced the sandwiches along with bottled water and a couple bags of potato chips in almost less time than it took Abby to collect her day pack from her room. She stuffed it all inside the pack except for one sandwich that Tanner held on to as he slipped the pack over his shoulder.

"It won't do any good for you to talk if I can't hear you over the rumbling of my own stomach," he said in reply to her amused glance, then nudged her out the door. Abby assumed he was hurrying to avoid letting everyone indoors watch his first ravenous bites, and she was right. Tanner had no more closed the door behind them when he unwrapped the package and sank his teeth into thick slices of ham and whole grain bread.

With a delighted laugh, she led the way down to the beach. By the time they'd left the garden behind and were making their way across the deep sand to a large flat rock at the water's edge, he'd finished the whole thing.

She climbed onto the rock and sat down facing the water as Tanner settled beside her. For several minutes, they just sat there, quietly sharing their enjoyment of a day so misty that the opposite shore was hidden from sight.

"There's a fabulous view from here," she said after a while. "You should have come down here yesterday when it was clear."

"You wouldn't let me," he said as he began to spread their lunch onto the flattest part of the rock.

"Don't give me that nonsense, Tanner." She took the sandwich he handed her without quite meeting his gaze, pretending to be occupied finding a comfortable position on the hard surface. "You've always done exactly what you wanted."

"Not always."

There was a quiet rebuke in his words that prevented her from speaking, and she knew what he was going to say long before the words came out.

"That night in Aspen, I wanted to come inside you more than I wanted to breathe. I don't think you've ever realized what it cost me to stop when I did."

Suddenly, she had to know why he'd done just that. Putting the sandwich aside, she lifted her gaze and let it be captured by his. She felt a familiar warmth, a sense of safety and wholeness of being that was always there when she let him inside, past her defenses. The feeling was one she'd denied herself over the years by the simple expedient of not meeting his gaze. In the past twenty-four hours, she'd become addicted to it.

"Why did you, Tanner? Why did you stop?"

"I thought you knew."

"I always assumed it was because I was a virgin," she said quietly, then looked away because there was only so much she could stand of letting him see into her soul. "I knew you were angry about that, that it was the reason you wouldn't go any further. Then I realized it wasn't that simple."

"When did you figure that out?"

"Yesterday, when you got angry after I suggested I might have had other lovers. I realize now that you wanted that part of me for yourself, that you always had." Cold bit at her fingers as they lay clasped across her knee, and she focused on that small discomfort in an effort to retain a sense of equilibrium. "If that part of you has never changed, then I have to believe there was another reason you stopped."

She had to wait until he unwrapped another sandwich and ate a few bites before he answered. When he did, he spoke to the waves that lapped twenty feet from the rock and didn't once turn to look at her. "I knew the first time I kissed you that I could easily lose my head over you. By the time I had you naked beneath me, I'd begun to realize I might lose my heart too." Without looking, he reached over and took her hand in his, twining their fingers with careful precision. "I think that when I discovered you were a virgin, I was so conscious of the fact that I might lose myself entirely in you that I grabbed that as an excuse to get away before it was too late."

The fact that his explanation was simply another angle on the "consequences" he'd stunned her with earlier didn't lessen its impact. If anything, it touched her even deeper because the more he said, the more she realized his commitment. It terrified her and thrilled her all in the same moment, leaving her shivering with a recognition of what Pandora must have felt when she opened the box.

Perhaps what he'd already shared made her brave, or maybe it was the frustration of being deprived of the joy she'd found in his arms that made her push for more, to learn more about this man at her side. Either way, she was about to ask what had made him change his mind when he picked up her sandwich and held it to her mouth. She accepted his silent entreaty to change the subject, and after eating in silence for several minutes, she began to tell him about Samuels before he had to ask again.

"I went to Scotland to follow up a lead I got on a woman who's been producing these wonderful sketches of the lochs around Dornie. They're pen and ink, and I thought they'd sell well in sets—originals, mind you. She hasn't gotten commercial enough for prints yet." Tanner screwed off the top of the water, and Abby took a long swallow before giving it back to him. "Anyway, I knew Samuels was on my trail because I'd spotted him at the hotel in Edinburgh. I was pretty sure he didn't know what I was after, though, and didn't worry about it when he followed me from the hotel. I went to the local castle, Eilean Donan, and then drove as far as I could up a dirt road on Loch Long to see if I could come up with any ideas of other views that might look well in a set of six or eight. I didn't figure he'd learn anything by following me up there."

"You're sure he followed you?"

"Hmm." She nodded and opened the bag of chips

he handed her. "He didn't have much of a chance at staying hidden as this is not a well-traveled road, even in the height of tourist season. I suppose I shouldn't have teased him, though. That's probably what made him do it."

"Do what, Abby?"

She heard the implacable note in his voice that meant he wasn't going to ask that question again. Still, she let him wait a little longer as she strung out the story. "After hiking around the hills for a bit, I decided to go for a walk along the shore. It was still light out, and I thought a view of the village of Conera across the loch might make another sketch." She waved a potato chip in the air at Tanner's explicit comment on her little walk. "Think what you want, Tanner, but I'd decided that if Samuels was stupid enough to follow me all day just to get a hint of what I was after, then he deserved to squirm a little. Anyway, I headed that direction and when he didn't follow, I figured he'd gotten fed up and left."

"Had he?"

"Absolutely. By the time I got back to where I'd left the car, it was nearly dark. Unfortunately, the air had been let out of all four tires." She quirked a knowing eyebrow at Tanner. "I deduced your employee had done the deed to get even with me for wasting his time."

Anger, dark and ominous, smoldered in Tanner's eyes, but his tone was mild as he urged her to continue. "Now's when you tell me about the dog."

She hurried through it, wanting to get it over because the surrounding mist suddenly made it seem too real, as though that single frightening night were happening all over again. "I had to walk back in the dark, the mist got heavy, and I got lost when I took the wrong turn off the road. The dog found me a couple of hours later."

She was shaking, and went readily into Tanner's arms as he shifted on the rock and pulled her close. He didn't ask her for anything more, and she didn't offer it. It was over and done with, and as he rocked her and crooned comforting words into her ear, she could believe that nothing would ever frighten her again.

It occurred to her then that Tanner wouldn't have to soothe her if he hadn't sanctioned Samuels's efforts in the first place. She shrugged out of his embrace and glared up at him. "Are you just sorry because this stunt got out of hand? If that's your thinking, then perhaps you should have been there to muzzle Samuels in Thailand when he told the airport authorities I was smuggling heroin. I suppose I'm lucky he didn't actually plant anything on me for them to find, because I'd still be there or dead, no thanks to your idiot employee."

The color washed out of his face as though someone had waved a magic wand, his eyes slammed shut, and he became as still as the rock they sat upon. He didn't try to speak or touch her or, it seemed, to breathe.

She'd shocked him, and was shocked in return. A suspicion that had been lurking in an obscure corner of her mind came forward, tugging a ray of hope in its wake. She hadn't liked thinking Tanner would condone Samuels's rather vicious streak, but she'd shrugged off his lack of protest as ignorance of all the facts. She'd imagined that Samuels had given his boss results without tarrying over the details, thus essentially letting Tanner off the hook.

She'd given Tanner the benefit of the doubt because

she hadn't wanted to believe otherwise. Because of the severity of the incidents, though, she hadn't been entirely successful in erasing them from her mind.

"This is the first time you've heard any of this, isn't it, Tanner?"

He opened his eyes then, and she saw what he'd been hiding, what he couldn't seem to control. Horror battled rage in their fiery depths, and the passion of his emotions was so strong that she would have been terrified if Tanner were any other man.

"I swear, Abby. I didn't know, not any of it." His voice was rough and scratchy, making each word sound like a major effort. "No one in my employ is supposed to interfere with you whatsoever. I made it plain three years ago that any dirty tricks were strictly between the two of us. Anything Samuels did, he did on his own."

He lifted her chin with the cuff of his hand, his touch a tender contrast to his fierce gaze. "How can you doubt me like you have and still want me to touch you, Abby? How can you bear to be near me while believing that I would allow someone to hurt you?"

She had to swallow over the lump in her throat before she could answer. "Deep inside, I've always known it wasn't anything to do with you. Maybe I hung on to it, though, because otherwise I wouldn't have had a score to even out."

"And that was so important?"

"Yes." She dipped her head to avoid the warm glitter of understanding in his gaze, but he forced it back up with a gentle nudge.

"Why, Abby?"

"Because it was the only thing we had between us, Tanner. If I couldn't blame you for Samuels's deeds, I doubt that I would have had the nerve to drag you all

the way to Ireland." Her hands curled around his forearm as though it were a lifeline. "I had no idea whether
you even remembered that night in Aspen, much less if
you were interested in taking up where we left off. I
had to have some excuse if everything went wrong—
pride and all that, you know."

The ghost of a smile touched his lips. "I haven't
stopped wanting you for three years, lass. My acting
skills must be better than I thought if you were that
uncertain of how I'd react to any invitation from you.
Haven't you figured out yet that I would have come to
Ireland even if you hadn't threatened to run me for
office?"

"Your secretary believed me."

"That's because she's had three years of scrambling
for airplane seats and whatnot every time I decided to
go chasing after you. You've got her well-conditioned."
Without waiting for any kind of a reply, he began stuff-
ing the leftovers and trash into the pack. Then he
jumped down onto the hard sand and held out a hand
as she followed. Side by side, they headed back to the
hotel.

They were over halfway there before she spoke.
"What are you going to do about Samuels?"

"I've already fired him—"

"You did?" She looked up at him in surprise. She'd
expected something along those lines the day before
when his rage had surfaced at the mere mention of an
incident, but she hadn't realized he'd do it before he
had the whole story out of her.

"Hmm." He snagged her hand and smiled down at
her. "Unfortunately, it seems I was a bit premature.
Now I'll have to look him up and make sure he under-
stands how badly he messed up."

"I didn't tell you about this so you could stage a macho get-even scene, Tanner."

"Don't worry, Abby. I won't do anything you wouldn't do in my position," he said, throwing her earlier words back at her. "Speaking of which, I never did get around to yelling at you, did I?"

"No, and now I don't have time to put up with it." She slid her hand from his and quickened her pace across the mist-soaked lawn. "I've got some calls to make. See you at dinner."

She was almost to the front door when she turned around and added, "Don't be too hard on Samuels. If you and I hadn't set such a terrible example, he would never have gotten the idea in the first place."

Tanner let her go without arguing, knowing it would only upset her to know just how macho he intended to get with Samuels. In the meantime, he decided to work off the edge of his aggression with a long run. Maybe by the time he ran four or five miles, he'd have figured out just how badly he could hurt the man without killing him.

It took eight miles followed by fifty laps in the heavily chlorinated pool before Tanner felt in reasonable control of his emotions. Back in his suite, he stripped off his bathing trunks and, yawning for no good reason other than his body clock was still disorganized, he went into his bathroom. The shower cubicle was fitted into a corner and was big enough to get the job done, but devoid of the excessive elbowroom offered by the bathtub. That meant Tanner had nowhere to hide as the stinging icicles blitzed his torso. He withstood the punishment until the idea of grabbing a quick nap had flown from his head, then reached out blindly to adjust the water temperature to something suited more to a human than a polar bear.

The sharp rap of knuckles against the glass enclosure made his hand slip on the handle. Before he could correct the error, he was bombarded by a hissing spray that was hot enough to parboil the skin from a tomato. Cursing loudly, he slammed a shoulder against the curved door and hopped out onto the blessedly cool tiles.

He looked up to see Abby grinning at him from where she lounged just inside the door, her arms crossed under her breasts and one ankle hooked across the other. Her silk robe was closed primly at her neck, and she'd wrapped a towel turban-style around her head.

"What's the matter, Tanner? Can't take the heat?"

He grabbed a towel and flipped it around his hips, then gingerly reached inside the cubicle to shut off the water before it flooded the sitting room or whatever was on the level below. When he looked back at her, she was still grinning.

"Dammit, Abby, if you don't want to make love to me, all you have to do is say so. I can do without having my testicles scorched." Or any other important parts, he muttered under his breath as he glanced down to his feet. They were a dull red and looked somewhat puffy. He was tempted to check under his towel for similar damage, but refrained. Grabbing a couple more towels from the rack, he threw them onto the floor to soak up the water.

"If you didn't want company," she said, "you should have locked the door." There was a definite note of humor catching at her silky drawl.

"Touché." He glared at her, doing his best to keep his own amusement submerged. It wouldn't do, he thought, to let her know how much he enjoyed it when she won a point. "Did you want anything in particular, or is this just a social call?"

He leaned a shoulder against the cool wall and let his gaze drift over her. The robe did nothing to hide her curves, and he thought he could see the faint outline of her nipples pushing at the thin barrier. They'd have to be hard to do that, he mused, and wondered what she'd do if he closed the gap between them to find out.

"I came for these." She pulled a set of keys from a pocket, and he recognized them as the ones he'd lifted from her room. "Just thought I'd let you know where they disappeared to."

He smiled lazily. "Too bad. I'd hoped you came over to force me to make love to you."

Her blush deepened, but her response was so flip that he wondered if it was the steamy bathroom causing her color to rise. "There's only an hour before dinner, Tanner."

"We can set the alarm."

"I just washed my hair. It's still wet."

"So's mine, but if we get under the blankets real fast, we won't catch cold."

"I have some more work to do." Her fingers curled around her elbows, and he thought her grin was becoming a trifle forced. "Besides, you gave me a lot to think about this afternoon. I'm still working on it."

"You want to talk about it?" He kept his voice mild so that she wouldn't know how close he was to taking her into the next room and stretching out with her on the bed—doubts and all.

"Talk to me, Abby," he said when she didn't answer.

She shook her head very slowly. "Maybe that's what's wrong, Tanner. All we seem to do is talk."

"Kissing you is hard on my control. Talking is safer."

The look of frustration on her face made him want to gather her into his arms and hold her until she wasn't thinking about anything at all. He straightened from the wall and was about to reach for her when she suddenly backed away. Tanner made himself stand quite still, and was relieved when she paused just outside the bathroom door.

"I won't hurt you, Abby," he said softly, then couldn't help the wry smile that kicked at one corner of his mouth. "At least, not like I did the last time. There's a certain amount of discomfort for a woman her first time, but I'll do everything I know to make it as easy as I can."

A soft hiss of breath reached his ears. She said, "I don't think I can do this, not with you."

"Why not me?"

"Because you want all of me, and I don't know if I want to give it to you. I don't even know if I can." She hesitated, then shook her head helplessly. "Maybe it would be easier with another man who won't expect what you do."

He held on to his sudden temper by a very slender thread. "Do us both a favor and don't talk about other men."

"Jealous?" A single eyebrow quirked in surprise.

"Possessive." He caught her startled gaze and held it. "You like that, don't you?"

"Yes." She reached blindly for something to hold on to, and her fingers curled around the edge of the door. "I thought you said talking was safer than kissing. To be absolutely honest, when you say things like that, my body doesn't feel much different than before when you were kissing me and I was burning up inside."

Again, it took an amazing amount of self-control not to go to her and put an end to the waiting. "Then I suppose we should postpone the kissing and the talking until at least one of us has some clothes on. Right now, the barriers between us are too fragile to trust. They might fall."

"Worse things could happen."

"I want you to be sure, not just aroused." He fisted his hands at his sides and took a deep, cleansing breath. "I want you to be very sure, because once we've made love, nothing will ever be the same."

Before she could respond to that, he said, "Now, why don't you go dry your hair and get dressed. We can meet in the bar for a drink before dinner."

She hesitated for so long, Tanner nearly changed his mind. Then she turned and left in such a hurry that he couldn't have caught her if he tried. The click of the bolt on the other side of the door canceled any notion he had of following, and with a long sigh, he pulled the towel from his hips and reached for his clothes.

Letting her run—or think she was running things— was his best strategy, Tanner assured himself as he dressed. Now that Abby had taken that first daring step of bringing the two of them together, he could afford the luxury of waiting for her to come to terms with a decision she'd already made. Despite what he'd said to her, he was fully aware she'd made up her mind about him and the consequences. All she had to do now was come to terms with it.

So long as he kept her in sight, it was only a matter of time before they began again the lovers' waltz.

SEVEN

A brilliant morning sun glinted off the Jaguar's silver hood, nearly blinding Tanner who watched impotently from his bedroom window as the car and the truck towing it rounded the bend in the drive and disappeared.

"That little witch!" A reluctant smile nudged at his lips, and he paused a moment to give Abby her due—admiration mixed with annoyance—before crossing to the phone and dialing the number of a local car rental company recommended by the hotel. By the time he'd finished explaining what he needed, he felt confident that he was, once again, two steps ahead of Abby.

The fact that she was already two hours south and pressing hard didn't alter that estimation, because Tanner had taken the precaution of warning Rory of Abby's possible flight when he'd briefed his cousin on the little Abby had shared about Yoshimoto. Rory had called from his car phone to report when Abby had left the hotel just after daybreak, and had updated Tanner ten minutes earlier with their mutual progress.

Recovering her keys had been the tip-off, but Tanner would have expected something like this in any case. It was just like Abby to resume their contest as though nothing more important was happening in their worlds, getting the jump on him even though the last thing he had on his mind was vying for merchandise.

Yes, he was ahead of her, but the smug satisfaction he'd felt while he was dressing and packing had been replaced by a vague feeling of embarrassment. He should have known better than to imagine she would leave without doing something to delay his pursuit. At least he was being smart enough to replace the car instead of trying to recover the Jaguar, which was likely to be booby-trapped in such a way as to cost him time, money, or a lot of both. Abby wouldn't have missed a trick like that, not after she'd gone to all the bother of spinning a story that had been convincing enough to persuade someone to tow a perfectly good car from a respectable hotel's parking lot without consulting the person responsible.

Not knowing the story could possibly even get him jailed. He decided not to chance it.

Tanner forced himself to go down to the dining room for breakfast while he waited the hour before the car was due to arrive. With Abby's three-hour head start to wherever she was going, he doubted he'd have time for lunch. Caution made him stop and peer through the French doors, and only when he was certain that Ms. Browning—their dinner companion the previous evening—was absent did he enter. He grabbed a peach off the buffet table in passing, and asked the waiter for coffee before taking a seat in the far corner with his back to the room. He wasn't in the mood for company. Neither, apparently, was the man at the next table who—in total disregard of the Anglo-Irish custom of mouthing the appropriate greeting to perfect strangers whose faces they remembered from the night before—presented Tanner with the back view of his shoulder and left shortly thereafter. Tanner eyed the full cup of coffee and half-finished breakfast the man had left and was wondering about his rush when his own solitude was disturbed.

"Oh, good. There you are!" A plump hand patted his shoulder, and Tanner had about two seconds to wipe the dismay from his face before Ms. Browning came into his field of vision. She stood expectantly beside the chair opposite him, a yellow-print polyester dress falling loosely over her ample curves. This morning, her carrot-red hair had been roughly tamed into something that looked to be a cross between a beehive and a bird's nest. Harlequin glasses fell from a blue crystal chain at her neck—a surprise because she'd been quite proud of the monocle she'd sported the night before—and there was a ring on her finger that looked like a piece of cement.

Tanner knew better than to imagine she was waiting for an invitation.

Swallowing a groan, he rose and went around the table to pull out her chair. By the time she was comfortable, he hadn't managed to think of an excuse to leave that wouldn't offend her—if that were possible—so he sat down and prayed the waiter would hurry with his coffee.

"I do hate eating breakfast alone. Don't you, Mr. Flynn?" He grunted, and Ms. Browning beamed with pleasure. "And where is that sweet Ms. Roberts this morning? Is she sleeping in?"

"I'm sure I wouldn't know, Ms. Browning. I didn't stop by her room on my way down."

"But I thought—" She interrupted herself mid-sentence, and the florid color in her cheeks gave Tanner a certain amount of satisfaction. When she grabbed the menu from the center of the table and hid behind it, he felt only a small twinge of remorse.

To be fair, it wasn't Ms. Browning's fault that she'd assumed he and Abby were sharing a room. Abby certainly hadn't done anything to dispel the impression that they were a couple in the most intimate sense of the word. In fact, she'd treated Tanner with a kind of casual teasing that had kept him on the edge of his chair all through dinner. The entertainment value of a courting couple hadn't been lost on Ms. Browning either.

Tanner hadn't been too surprised to find Abby chatting with Ms. Browning when he'd joined her in the cellar bar the previous evening. Abby simply wasn't the kind of person who would sit alone when there was someone else to pass the time with. He'd often admired that openness in her that allowed her to make friends with little more in common than a shared language.

Until last night, though, when she'd deliberately turned their intimate duo into a cozy threesome.

She'd started off by introducing the older woman as a retired schoolteacher from Derry who had, by the way, third cousins in California, then proceeded to coax details from Ms. Browning, who admitted early on that she'd never once met the cousins or gone to California. Tanner hadn't gotten suspicious until Abby had persisted in encouraging the woman to talk about everything from herself to her country. Ms. Browning hadn't needed much encouragement, although Tanner had to give her credit for making a token effort at not joining them for dinner.

Abby wouldn't hear of it. In fact, she'd kept the respectable Ms. Browning latched to her side throughout the evening. Medieval knights could have learned a thing or two from Abby about the effective use of shields. She'd wielded Ms. Browning with a skill that didn't falter once—right up to the point after coffee when she'd suggested Tanner escort Ms. Browning to her room. By the time he'd returned from that gentlemanly chore, Abby had locked herself safely inside her suite.

Tanner supposed he couldn't blame Ms. Browning for assuming he wanted company for breakfast. He cleared his throat and chose a topic guaranteed to bring Ms. Browning out from behind the menu. "You mentioned last night that you were going to explore the Rathmullan Priory today."

She peeked at him over the top of the card, then apparently decided to accept the olive branch, because she flipped the card aside and nodded vigorously. "They call it a priory, but it was really a friary—there is a difference, you know. It has a connection to the hotel, through Bishop Knox—the Knoxes were the original owners of this place, as I'm sure you were aware—and he converted . . ."

During the next thirty minutes, Tanner discovered a remarkable facility in himself for being able to nod and toss in the odd "uh-huh" or "you don't say" at just the right moment, all without diverting his thoughts far from Abby and the look that was going to be on her face when he caught up with her.

A feeling of mellow anticipation seeped through him as he contemplated the day ahead. There was nothing he liked better than a leisurely drive through the Irish countryside on a gloriously bright day like the one that was shaping up outside.

He felt so good that when Ms. Browning ran out of things to say about Rathmullan, he asked about the hunk of cement on her finger.

In the ensuing fifteen minutes, Tanner learned enough about the toppling of the Berlin Wall to fill a textbook.

Abby drove without worrying about schedule, delighting in the secluded feel of narrow roads that were alternately bordered by stone walls and deep, impenetrable hedgerows. Today, all she had to do was take care of a little business in a village north of Tralee, then get to the hotel outside of Killarney and wait for Tanner to show up.

The next day, they'd visit a nearby woolen factory where she expected Tanner to buy several dozen hats like the sample one she'd received the night before. It would be a small enough purchase, but there wasn't a huge demand for Irish fishermen's hats in Phoenix. The Pacific Northwest, on the other hand, would provide a natural market for the water-resistant wool hat. She wondered if Tanner would see the potential for his catalogue sales—or if she'd have to beat him over the head with it. Subtly, of course. Otherwise, all the trouble she'd gone to in setting up the hat as a red herring would be a total waste.

She never considered that Tanner wouldn't be on hand to go to the factory with her the next day. She'd certainly left a wide enough trail for him to follow. If he missed the crumpled note in the waste basket with the Killarney hotel's name and address, he'd almost certainly discover a surprising willingness in the manager of Rathmullan House to reveal the forwarding address she'd so considerately left behind. If either of those failed, he could always call her office in Phoenix and get an update from her secretary.

No, she didn't want to lose him, nor was it indecision over their personal involvement that had inspired her early-morning flight from Rathmullan. It was strictly business. He'd realize that—even if he didn't have the details—and he'd follow because this hide-and-seek game they played was as much a habit as it was a challenge. And until the sale of Desert Reef was final—which would be soon, if Sandra came through as she'd promised when they spoke the previous afternoon—then Abby had to go on as she had before, the only difference being that she was now buying for a shop that wouldn't be hers in another few weeks.

Nevertheless, it was still hers . . . which necessitated keeping on her toes and at least three steps ahead of Tanner. For the moment, at least one of those steps translated to a few hours' breathing space, due almost entirely to Tanner's transportation glitch.

Thanks to an early-morning call from Yoshimoto, she was on the road nearly an hour earlier than planned. The call was the second he'd made since receiving her fax, and hadn't varied much in content from what he'd told her in Phoenix—except to include Tanner in his threats.

That was unfortunate. She would have rather not told Tanner anything about her problems with Yoshimoto, and now she'd probably have to spill everything before they went back to Phoenix. Hopefully, though, she'd have the sale of Desert Reef concluded and it would no longer be an issue.

Abby supposed she should have consulted Tanner about the fax, but she couldn't see where telling Yoshimoto that she was selling Desert Reef to Tanner was really any of Tanner's business—particularly as it was a piece of fiction in the first place. Her logic had been that Yoshimoto wouldn't dare threaten Tanner the way he'd done with Sandra, thus creating a lull which would allow Abby to conclude negotiations with Sandra while Yoshimoto counted his losses.

At least, that was the way it was supposed to have worked, and it had, if only to the extent that he was now off Sandra's back. The fact that it hadn't succeeded in cowing Yoshimoto totally was something she'd deal with when they went back to Phoenix.

In the meantime, she had all of Ireland to share with Tanner Flynn, and she intended to enjoy every second of it. Whether they went home as friends or "true" lovers was something that would happen whether she worried about it or not. Tanner's attempt to control things with talk of decision making had clouded an otherwise simple issue.

Abby hadn't waited three years for Tanner only to let him slip through her fingers now. If there were consequences to be faced, they would do that the same way they made love: Together.

Smiling despite the dark clouds that threatened from the west, Abby patted herself on the back for thinking of calling the garage to tow away Tanner's car. Acting the part of Mr. Flynn's secretary, she'd informed them that Mr. Flynn had experienced severe difficulties with the steering and suggested the car be examined by a mechanic before it was returned to service. As for Mr. Flynn, he would continue his journey by other means.

She spent a brief minute wondering how long it would take Tanner to organize other transportation before her thoughts strayed once again to Yoshimoto and his threats. Sly references to "unfortunate accidents" and "unforeseen business losses" sounded ridiculously melodramatic when you came right down to it. Yoshimoto, she was convinced, was all talk and no action. Otherwise, he would have acted before now—which was the real reason she'd dismissed his threats as empty words.

Still, she'd rather not have to put up with his threats any longer. Making a mental note to call her office and tell her secretary that Yoshimoto was not on the list of people with access to her whereabouts, Abby concentrated on the narrow road and hoped the hay wagon coming toward her wasn't so wide that she'd have to retreat.

Tanner didn't know which was worse: The increasing lack of visibility or the squeak of the windshield wipers that were proving less than capable of doing their job. The steering wheel fought his hands as yet another unseen lake-size pool of rainwater reached out from the curbside of the road and tried to suck the tiny car into its depths. He downshifted into second, and wondered how many more dunkings the car could take before it drowned.

The wheel jumped again, and for the hundredth time that afternoon, Tanner cursed Abby and her miserable thoroughness. She'd known that there was only one car hire agency recommended by the hotel and had obviously spoken to them before his own call. The car he'd gotten in place of the Jaguar was little more than a box on wheels with an engine only slightly more powerful than the one inside the lawn mower he'd noticed grooming the lawns of Rathmullan House that morning. If he hadn't been in such a hurry to get on the road, he would have sent it back for something more reasonable.

Now, after eight long hours of coaxing the thing along country roads and occasional stretches of dual carriageway, Tanner wasn't certain the lawn mower wouldn't have been a more sensible choice. At least then he'd only be getting drenched instead of being wedged inside the impossibly small interior with his knees up to his ears and his nose pushed flat against the windshield in an attempt to see through it in the driving rain. What had started out as a glorious morning had, by small gestures and steps, evolved into a dreary, waterlogged Irish afternoon.

The mobile phone on the passenger seat rang, and Tanner grabbed it without moving his nose out of position. "Yeah?"

"Where in God's name are you? You'll miss tea if you don't get here soon, Tanner." Rory's voice came through loud and clear on the state-of-the-art telephone. At least the agency hadn't skimped on that requirement.

"If this sorry excuse for a car doesn't learn how to swim, I'll miss dinner too." He leaned his head back a few inches and swiped at the misting windshield with his forearm. A sign heralding the outskirts of Killarney came into view before the window fogged over again. He used his other arm to clear it this time, and checked again to make sure the defroster was switched on its highest setting.

"I got you a room next door to Abby's," Rory said. "They're both on the fifth floor. Nice big rooms they are, too, but I think they're giving everyone who shows up the deluxe treatment. The hotel's closing for the winter next week, and it's nearly empty now."

"Connecting?"

"Sorry?"

"The rooms, Rory. Are they connecting?" Tanner didn't care how empty the hotel was or about anything else but the essentials.

"Sorry, lad. Either they don't have such niceties, or the management was unwilling to subject such a sweet-looking lass to the complications such an arrangement might, er . . . well, engender." Rory obviously couldn't resist emphasizing the "gender."

Tanner hated it when Rory talked like the punctilious civil servant he'd guarded in one of his earlier incarnations. "See what you can do about figuring out what she's got on her slate for tomorrow. I don't want to spend another day playing catch-up."

"I've already looked through her car, and there wasn't anything useful. I suppose I could search her room while you're at dinner, but I feel like I'm invading her privacy without cause. I'm supposed to be protecting Abby, not spying on her."

"Just do it and don't worry about Abby's privacy. *She* didn't have her car towed away this morning," Tanner growled.

Rory just laughed, then described the changes he'd made in his appearance which were designed to fool Abby.

Tanner wasn't impressed. Dying blond hair brown

and putting on a pair of glasses didn't sound like enough change, but he assumed his cousin knew what he was talking about. Telling Rory to send out a lifeboat if he didn't show up within the next thirty minutes, he tossed the phone aside and concentrated on finding his way through a city which—given the number of multilingual tax-free signs he saw posted in shop fronts—had embraced tourism with the appetite of lions at the Coliseum.

Tanner spotted Rory tucked up to the brass-trimmed bar in the lounge, but it had taken two sweeps of the room before he'd come back to the bland-looking man in the travel-worn suit and wire-rim glasses. His hair, a light shade of brown, was combed straight back from his forehead and shone with the kind of oil older men used instead of mousse, and the mustache drooping from his upper lip looked as though it needed a good trimming. The disguise worked because it was simple enough to be believable and managed to alter his profile entirely. By the time Abby caught on—*if* she caught on—Tanner hoped to know enough about Yoshimoto to neutralize him.

He blinked once at Rory's amazing transformation, then ignored him because Abby was at a nearby table, keeping company with another man—about ten years old, from the look of him. She glanced up from the cards she held fanned in her hand, saw him, then checked the time on her wristwatch. When she looked at him again, her eyes were aglow with mischief.

"You're late, Tanner."

"I overslept. You should have awakened me when

you . . . left," he said, thinking that accusing her of sneaking out was a bit harsh for young ears.

It occurred to him that he'd rarely seen her looking better, and wondered what sparked the inner excitement that made her eyes shine like liquid silver against the background of the amethyst sweater she wore. The cowl neck lapped softly against the upper curve of her breasts, and there was an almost imperceptible irregularity in the way her chest rose and fell with each breath.

She wasn't as calm as she pretended.

"I had to find someone else to play with," she said, indicating the youth sitting opposite her. Between them, a candle burned deep inside a golden bowl of artistically sculpted crystal, giving off more atmosphere than light and throwing in the illusion of warmth as a bonus.

Tanner manfully kept himself from glaring at the boy who looked patently disgusted at the interruption. "May I get you two a drink?"

The kid shook his head, then put down a yellow card with the word "Reverse" on it.

Abby said, "A sherry, please," and looked at her own cards with a worried frown. She was picking up another card from the stack on the table when he turned to get their drinks.

Rory had disappeared in the few seconds that Tanner's back had been turned, and Tanner figured he'd gone upstairs to invade Abby's privacy. He ordered Abby's sherry and an Irish whiskey for himself, and realized Rory hadn't been kidding about the lack of clientele in the hotel. Apart from the three couples and a foursome that were scattered around the elegantly appointed lounge, he'd seen only half a dozen other people since checking in and he couldn't be sure those weren't staff. It appeared that Rory would have to eat in his room in order to keep his face out of Abby's line of sight, Tanner mused as he carried the drinks back to the table.

He was just in time to see the youth slap down a multicolored wild card followed by Abby's groan of defeat.

"That's two games even, miss," he said, using the title all proper schoolchildren used when addressing virtually any woman in a more mature age bracket who wasn't family. "I don't suppose you have time for a tiebreaker?" He looked at Abby with the soulful eyes of a puppy begging to "go walkies."

"One more game, Elliot," she said, shuffling the cards. "Then I need to spend some time with Mr. Flynn. I'm dying to know what happened to his flash motor."

Flash motor? Tanner thought. Abby's language adaptation was better than his. He relaxed back in his chair as Elliot gave him a curious look.

"What kind of flash motor, sir?"

"A Jaguar."

"You lost a Jaguar?" Elliot's eyes were round with a combination of dismay and disbelief. "When? Where? How?"

"This morning, just outside of Rathmullan, and I'm not sure how." Tanner didn't disillusion the boy by admitting it technically hadn't been his car in the first place. His ears picked up something that sounded suspiciously like a snicker, but he couldn't tell for sure over the sound of the cards being dealt.

Without taking her eyes off her cards, Abby said, "All's well that ends well."

"Meaning?"

"You got here, didn't you?"

He reached out a long arm and lifted her chin with his knuckles until she had no choice but to look at him. "The car I was forced to drive the length of Ireland would make a Volkswagen bug look like a luxury sedan. The creaking you heard when I entered was my knees. They're still coming out of shock." He figured she was biting her lip to keep from laughing.

"Small, huh?"

He nodded. "My nose kept hitting the windshield. It was slow too."

"Did you check under the hood to see what the problem was?"

"I was afraid to." He dropped his hand and took a soothing taste of one of Ireland's finest staples. The single malt whiskey sent out signals of contentment all the way from his toes to his nose. He smiled as though he meant it, and realized he did. "The rain might have drowned the hamsters inside, and then where would I be?"

"You brought hamsters, sir?" Elliot asked. "May I see them?"

Abby's head dipped nose first toward the table as helpless giggles overtook her. Tanner pretended he didn't notice, and explained patiently to Elliot that the hotel did not, in fact, allow animals of any kind inside. Elliot was disappointed, but more than willing to revert to discussion of the Jaguar.

When Abby lifted her head, her eyes were teary from laughter and her nose looked as though it had met up with the same windshield as Tanner's had. He pulled a handkerchief from his breast pocket and offered it to her.

Abby took the handkerchief, thinking that she'd never seen this delightfully whimsical side of Tanner and wondering how she'd known it was there. Because she had simply known, she realized, somewhere deep inside her where hopes and dreams lay protected from reality's harsh perspective. It wasn't that the Tanner Flynn she'd always known was entirely humorless, but he'd always carried with him an aura of reserve that even her most outrageous teasing hadn't seemed to penetrate.

That reserve was gone, at least for the time being. Abby wanted to know how to banish it forever.

She dried her eyes without worrying about staining the pristine cloth, thankful that she'd once again eschewed mascara. Yes, she knew it made her eyes look bigger, but the little applicator wand was forever poking her in the eye. She was about to blow her nose when it occurred to her that the sensitive nerve endings on the tips of her fingers had been sending her an urgent message. She sniffled and brought the handkerchief to eye level for a closer inspection.

The hem was turned in double and hand-stitched—very nicely too—and the linen looked as though it had been woven with the kind of care that simply couldn't happen with machines.

Tanner had a distinctly suspicious look in his eyes when she caught his gaze. "Where'd you get this?" she asked. No sense beating around the bush, not if there was half a chance that Tanner's lack of reserve might extend to telling what amounted to trade secrets.

"My pocket."

She scowled. "You know what I mean."

He hesitated, then shrugged. "I suppose it doesn't matter, not anymore."

It only hurt a bit, his casual assumption that their competition was over. Then she remembered it still had a few weeks to run and felt the reassuring warmth seep through her. "So where did you find this, Flynn, and why haven't you been selling them?"

"My aunt sends me a half dozen every Christmas. I've never asked where she got them."

"It's not like you to miss a trick like this," she said, inspecting the fine Irish linen one more time before using it for the intended purpose. She stuffed it into the waistband of her calf-length skirt and smoothed the matching sweater back over her hips. "It never occurred to me when I chose Ireland for this—" She hesitated, remembering they weren't alone, and filled the blank with something innocuous. "When I chose Ireland for this vacation, I guess I didn't think about your family. Are there many that you keep in touch with?"

"A few." One corner of his mouth kicked upward, and she couldn't decide whether he was laughing at the word "vacation" or if there was something particularly funny about the way she'd brought up the subject of his relatives.

"It's your turn to start, miss." Elliot had apparently given up on getting any more Jaguar-related details, so Abby let Tanner's uninformative response get by—for the moment—and slapped a red four on top of a yellow one.

Five minutes and an ignominious loss later—thanks, in no small part, to Tanner and the way her skin tingled whenever he was near—she watched Elliot jog across the room to rejoin his parents.

"I hope he doesn't think I lost on purpose." She looked up to meet Tanner's warm gaze. "Kids like him hate winning by default."

"I suspect Elliot didn't care about winning or losing as much as he did about playing cards with a beautiful woman."

The compliment took her by surprise, and she instinctively ducked it. "He would have deserted me for your hamsters without a second thought. Besides, Elliot is too young to care what a woman looks like so long as she can play cards."

Tanner grinned, and there was a rumble of laughter in his voice when he said, "What's wrong, Abby? Is it the compliment that makes you uncomfortable, or the fact that you aren't sure I meant it?"

"Get off it, Tanner." She took a sip of sherry and wished she'd ordered something stronger. "The women you seem to spend most of your time with are always drop-dead gorgeous. Compared to them, cute is the best rating I'd get."

"Cute looks good on you," he said agreeably, "but that's not what I'm talking about." His expression went strangely soft, and when he looked at her, she felt as though he was trying to make her see herself through his eyes. "I never consciously realized you were beautiful until that night in Winnipeg when I saw you playing dominoes with that old man. It was St. Patrick's Day, and everyone else in the room was dancing and drinking and carrying on, and there you were, sitting with a man probably three times your age and looking as though you were having the time of your life."

She remembered that night clearly, partly because of Harry, but also because she remembered every single encounter she'd had with Tanner in the past few years. She'd made certain to keep out of his way that night, and had been rewarded with the excellent company of a man who, for lack of a better description, had "been there, seen it, and done it" and hadn't stopped yet.

"His name is Harry," she said, "and you're right. I was having a ball."

"It showed. You were sitting in front of the fire, and at first I thought the glow that surrounded you was from the flames."

"How do you know it wasn't?" she asked, feeling as though it was Christmas as Tanner revealed yet another side of himself.

"Because it's there every time you smile, even when there isn't a fire in sight."

"Oh." She swallowed air, and wondered why breathing was suddenly so hard. Then he changed the subject, and she nearly stopped breathing altogether.

"I should spank you for what you did to the Jaguar."

"You won't, though." She knew it wasn't a trick of the light that made his eyes suddenly darken.

He leaned his forearms on the table and spoke very softly so there was no chance of being overheard in the hushed confines of the nearly empty room. "If you ever pull another stunt like that, I'll get even, Abby. I'll take you somewhere private and turn you over my knee and then—"

"You wouldn't!" Heat suffused her cheeks as her imagination took hold.

He went on as though he hadn't heard her. His voice dropped to a husky drawl that sent a lightning bolt of heat straight through her. "I'll do exactly what I wish, lass, and after you get over being frightened at not being the one in control, you'll realize that there's pleasure in being vulnerable. I'll pet you and touch you in ways that will make you want to scream and cry and beg for more. And when my fingers are slick with your response and you're a breath away from losing your mind—" He paused and shook his head. "When you're that close, lass, I'll carry you into the bathroom and let you sizzle under a cold shower."

"What!" she squeaked, then looked guiltily around the room. Fortunately, no one was paying them any unusual attention. "You wouldn't really, would you?"

"Touch you like that? Of course I would."

The heat that pooled between her legs filled her with a kind of reckless daring she hadn't known she was capable of. Abby licked her lips and leaned so close, she could feel the heat of his breath on her mouth. "I was referring to the bit about the shower."

His eyes darkened until they were nearly black. "If I were you, I'd think twice about stealing my car again."

She decided she would think about it. Very seriously. Her attention shifted to her nipples that were hard and throbbing, and she started to lift a hand to soothe them before she realized where she was and what she was doing.

"What are you doing to me, Tanner?"

"It's called foreplay, Abby. Do you like it?" His heart pounded hard in his chest, and he watched, fascinated, as her pink tongue slid across her lips before disappearing again. He'd deliberately set out to arouse her with the erotic consequences a spanking had suggested, but hadn't counted on his own almost painful response.

He hadn't missed the slight movement of her hand, and knew exactly what she'd almost done. If she'd actually touched herself, he was certain his control would have lasted only as long as it took to get her behind a closed door. Taking slow, deep breaths, he eventually managed to rein in his thundering heart.

Realizing she still hadn't answered him, he did it for her. "I can see that you do like it. I'm glad. It will make the waiting that much more . . . interesting."

"I think . . . I want . . ."

He interrupted because she wanted the same damn thing he did and to hell with the consequences. "Let's go in to dinner, lass. Between breakfasting with Ms Browning and digging lunch out of a box that kept upending between my legs, I think I've earned a decent meal."

Abby put her hand into the one he held out to her and knew he'd been wrong about what he'd said the day before, when he'd told her nothing would ever be the same once they made love.

Everything had already changed beyond recognition, even if she was the only one who realized it.

EIGHT

The starkly erotic atmosphere of the lounge didn't stay with them through the five-course dinner. Tanner made sure of that by drawing the conversation along lines that were deliberately nonsexual. He wanted Abby to make a decision that was based on their future and not a passing arousal, and he felt guilty for having deliberately stoked that wanting.

So they talked about Ireland and the parts each liked best, and about the sales tax that was nearly double any similar tax they'd seen in the States. When she asked, he told her a little about his relatives in Ireland, beginning with his aunt Mary who lived south of Cork and ran a bed and breakfast. There were other aunts and uncles, too, as well as a few dozen cousins, scattered all across the country but not out of touch. Aunt Mary, bless her heart, made sure they all remembered they were part of a family, Tanner included. For obvious reasons, Rory's name never came up.

By the time they'd finished dessert, Abby looked as relaxed as he'd ever seen her and he himself was feeling distinctly mellow. He liked the vaguely unfamiliar sensation, and marveled at the range of emotions she was capable of evoking in him.

"I noticed a dominoes set in the lounge," he said as the waiter arranged the heavy silver coffee pot alongside the sugar and milk, then flicked a crumb from the tablecloth in parting. "Do you play often, or was that night with the old man a one-off?"

"That was a first. Harry taught me everything I know about the game." Abby stirred milk into her coffee, and they both watched as the vanilla/chocolate swirl dissolved into a shade of caramel. When she looked up again, Tanner thought he detected a hint of mischief in her gaze. "He would have taught you, too, if you'd asked."

"I thought the idea of huddling with Harry by the fire was to keep me at a safe distance."

"You and everyone else." She grinned. "It worked a treat, didn't it?"

He acknowledged her point with a solemn nod. "You've gotten quite adept at fending off rowdies and anyone else you want to avoid. I've always wondered what you said to that oaf in Anchorage who wouldn't leave you alone." The incident in question had happened soon after that night in Aspen, just one of the many times over the years that Tanner had gone out of his way to be right where Abby was. The fact that he'd managed to ace her out of a collection of native carvings had been a bonus.

That night, though, he'd been more concerned with the man who was bothering Abby. The hotel bar had been stretched to bulging with off-duty Air Force officers, oil riggers just in from the fields, and wide-eyed big game hunters from the Lower 48. Several of the predominantly male crowd had made overtures to Abby, and they'd all been turned away with a polite smile.

What had worried Tanner was a plaid-shirted bear of a man who didn't believe she meant it. Tanner had tried to let Abby handle the situation because he knew better than to interfere . . . and because he didn't have any right. But he could feel her annoyance clear across the room, and had just decided to get in the man's face when Abby made her own move. Taking a handful of the plaid, she hauled him down to where she could whisper in his ear. The man left the bar moments later, after sneaking a glance toward Tanner's corner without making eye contact.

"I told him," Abby explained now, "that you were out on a pass from a local mental institution where you'd been locked up after castrating your wife's lover. As your doctor, I was monitoring your behavior in a public setting." Her grin broadened as Tanner shifted uncomfortably in his chair. "I told him I was a little worried, because you had become quite possessive of me."

"At least it wasn't a total fib."

"Is that why you followed me today?"

He considered the question, then nodded. "That, and because I didn't want you to think I'd lost interest in our little competition. As I didn't know I was coming to Ireland in time to prepare a shopping list, the only thing I can do is try to keep up with you. It seems that this time, though, you have a serious advantage over me."

"Get real, Tanner. Nearly all of your shopping coups have consisted of finding out what I'm doing and getting there first. I don't see where anything's changed." She reached into a black satin-covered evening bag and pulled out a credit card. It took him a minute to realize it was his.

"When did you nick that?"

"Last night when I repossessed my keys. When I remembered your track record for getting lost, I thought it would behoove me to have it handy to celebrate my wins. What do you say—loser buys dinner?"

"You don't think the personal situation between us is complicated enough already without bringing business into it?" He cocked his head and thought about how many other ways he'd rather spend his time than chasing Abby all over Ireland.

"Maybe I just want to have something to talk about over dinner that won't scorch the ears off the waiter."

"Is that why you kept Ms. Browning so close last night, because you were afraid I'd spend the evening trying to sway your decision making?"

Abby took a sip of coffee, then pushed the half-empty cup aside. "No, Tanner, Ms. Browning was a delaying tactic. Last night, I was still under the impression I had a choice about us."

"And now?"

"And now that I've had time to think, I know better." She met his gaze, and hers was surprisingly steady. "I asked you to come to Ireland for strictly personal reasons. Nothing has changed to make me regret that decision, not even your insistence that there will be consequences."

"You're saying you can accept them?"

She shook her head. "Only that they don't matter. I want to make love with you, Tanner. It's the one thing I've been certain about all along."

"You're absolutely sure?" he asked softly, pushing

her right up against it because there would be no going back once it had begun, not this time.

"I'm sure." She blinked once, then added, "I would have never started this otherwise."

Her certainty filled him with the kind of pleasure that he'd only known on very special occasions, and none of those times came close to this in importance. He reached across the table and captured her hand. "There's something you should know about me before we go any further."

"What's that?" she asked, then tilted her head to one side as though something had just occurred to her. "It's not anything to do with those other women, is it?"

"In a way, yes." His grip tightened on hers as she tried to pull away. "Do you recall that discussion we had about assumptions?"

"I remember that I had trouble following it." She smiled tremulously. "I was still reeling from the rather straightforward way you told me to expect more than a single climax when we made love. Are you trying to tell me now that you were just teasing?"

"On the contrary. I was trying to warn you." His breath caught in his chest at the sudden heat in her eyes. "When a man has been celibate for as long as I have, it's safe to assume his first climax will be fairly shattering."

Her eyes sparkled with mischief, but the regret on its fringes didn't escape him. "What's it been, Tanner? A week, maybe two?"

"Three." He paused to look around the room, then caught her gaze before she'd had time to blink. "That's three years, Abby, not weeks."

"Oh." A long silence stretched between them, then

she turned her hand until their palms were together. "In that case, Tanner, let's make sure we get it right. It would be such a waste if we'd suffered all this time for nothing."

He laughed aloud at her impudence, then caught his breath as the roller coaster his emotions rode soared out of control.

Abby left Tanner organizing after-dinner drinks in the bar while she went back to her room to freshen up. Now that they'd reached an understanding, the need for hurry had diminished in the face of their enjoyment of the prelude. Each moment was to be savored, every sensation prolonged.

Each moment apart, therefore, was a hideous waste. Abby picked up a lipstick and touched it to her lips with a kind of impatience that was as frustrating as it was exciting. Had it not been for the moment she spared to look at her reflection and see the shine on her nose, she wouldn't have reached for the powder and wouldn't have noticed there was something not quite right about the way her personal things were arranged on the marble counter.

Forgetting the powder, she went back into the bedroom with its king-size bed at one end and an arrangement of Danish-looking chairs and table at the other, and carefully scanned the room. She could tell from the way that the middle dresser drawer was in perfect alignment with the others that someone had searched her room. She'd left the drawer open half an inch, just as she'd put her briefcase at a slight angle to the chair, and the angle was now doubled.

She grinned and wondered how Tanner had gotten

her key . . . or if somewhere along the way he'd learned how to jimmy a lock. Either way, she was pleased she'd gone to the trouble of taking precautions. Now that she knew *he* knew her shopping plan for the next day, she could quit holding her breath. Thanks to a little devious planning, he'd be too busy gloating over his hats to guess she'd been after something else all along.

She couldn't wait to see the look on Tanner's face when he realized he'd been had.

Abby was congratulating herself for putting all her really important materials in the hotel safe when she noticed an envelope on the table. Picking it up, she looked at the front and saw her name written in very precise block letters. A shiver of disquiet flitted up her spine as she remembered that the last time she'd seen similar writing had been on a note from Yoshimoto.

"How on earth did he know where I was?" she said aloud, then tsked as she remembered the trail she'd left for Tanner. Yoshimoto had probably called Rathmullan House and gotten the information the same way Tanner had, which would have given him enough time to express the letter over from Phoenix.

Flipping it unopened into the trash, she headed toward the door. She had no intention of letting Yoshimoto's strong-arm tactics spoil the evening ahead, and reading the note would probably do just that. It was far more interesting to contemplate how the letter had ended up in her hotel room.

The logistics were certainly possible, she decided as she pulled the door shut and headed down the hall. But it didn't explain why the hotel had put it in her room instead of calling to let her know it had arrived. Or why the express packaging had been removed. Probably some eager beaver at the front desk, she decided. Now how was she going to keep Tanner on track without giving Yoshimoto the same opportunities?

She hadn't come up with a solution by the time she got to the top of the stairs and noticed the nearby elevator was stopped at her floor. It didn't take any major effort to talk herself into riding down the six floors to ground level. She pulled open the door of the World-War-II-era cage, stepped inside, and pushed the button for the ground floor. When nothing happened, she checked to make sure the door was fully shut and saw something wedged into the corner. A firm tug was all it took to dislodge the obstruction, and the inner doors slid shut a moment before the elevator began moving downward. Abby straightened with an empty matchbox in her hand with Rathmullan House pictured on one side.

"Odd," she said aloud, and was wondering which of the handful of that night's lodgers had also been a guest at Rathmullan House when the lights went out.

"Now what?" Her exasperation echoed in the still-moving cage as Abby tried to remember if the controls were on the right or the left. She was just reaching out when the elevator floated to a stop. She heard, rather than saw, the inner door sliding open. Tentatively— because in the pitch dark she wasn't entirely convinced the elevator hadn't stopped between floors—she edged forward and felt for the outer door. Her palm found cold, smooth metal. Reassured, she gave it a little push. It swung into a darkness that was only slightly less thick than the variety inside the cage.

Abby knew which darkness she preferred. Thankful that she'd never quite gotten the hang of high heels— and, therefore, wasn't wearing any—she shuffled out of the elevator and let the door swing shut behind her. Muted noises from the public rooms reinforced her memory of the layout of the ground floor. Turning as close to ninety degrees left as she could manage, she clutched her handbag under one arm, held the other arm straight out in case a wall reached out and bit her, and began walking.

Half a dozen steps later, just when Abby thought she was getting the hang of it, the floor disappeared from beneath her feet and she pitched headfirst into the void.

Tanner had left the candlelit lounge behind and was already racing down the pitch black hall toward the guest-room elevators when he heard Abby's scream. He didn't question how he knew it was her. He just ran toward it, clutching in one hand the bowl of light he'd taken from one of the tables and in the other, a backup box of matches. Rounding a corner, he sprinted through a black corridor toward the staircase and took the carpeted steps three at a time. They were shallow and about ten feet wide, and there was a landing halfway up big enough to accommodate a roomful of furniture . . . which was a good thing, because with Abby sprawled in the middle of it, it was nice to have somewhere to land his feet that didn't include her face.

Checking his mad dash with a solid bump against the wall, Tanner dropped to his knees beside her. He swung the candle down her body, reminding himself not to touch her, yet so very desperate to do so—if only to reassure himself she was still alive.

She was on her back, and a quick perusal showed none of her limbs was sticking out in an odd direction.

There wasn't any blood, either, at least, not that he could see. And he could tell by the rise and fall of her chest that she was breathing more or less okay.

None of which meant she hadn't broken her neck. He held the light to her face and discovered she was watching him.

"Hey, buddy, can you spare a light?"

He opened his mouth to object to her flippant greeting, then snapped it shut when he realized that was her way of telling him she wasn't hurt. He would have preferred a simple "I'm okay," but nothing with Abby was ever simple.

"You screamed, madam?" he said in his best Jeeves imitation.

"Sorry about that. The stairs kind of snuck up on me in the dark." A chuckle escaped her lips. "Good of you not to trample me, Tanner. I have to admit to being a bit worried when a herd of elephants started charging this way."

"If you didn't want me to hurry, you should have pitched your scream differently. As it was, I thought I detected a slightly urgent note." He put the candle down near her head, the extra matches in his pocket, and took a deep breath in an effort to dismiss the case of shakes rolling through him.

"The next time I fall down a flight of stairs, I'll keep that in mind."

Tanner decided he'd had enough jokes. Bending closer, still without touching her, he said, "I need a little reassurance here, Abby. Are you certain you're all right?"

"I'm dented, not broken, Tanner. Trust me, I've taken worse falls than this on the ski slope."

"Then get up before I call the ski patrol. God

knows how many other fools there are in this hotel
who don't know any better than to wander around
when the electricity is off. We don't need for this to be
the first layer of a major pileup."

He waited until she started moving on her own,
then—convinced that she was not, in fact, paralyzed
from the neck down—slipped his hands under her
shoulders to help her. When she was sitting upright, he
eased his back against the wall and dragged her onto
his lap. When she didn't cry out or moan or anything
so frightening, he figured the only real damage was to
his overall life span. She'd knocked about ten years off
that.

"*This* fool," she said, "preferred wandering around
to being stuck in the elevator. If I'd known I wasn't on
the ground floor, my spirit of adventure would have
been somewhat tempered. I might even have had second thoughts about coming out of that elevator at all."
She wiggled her butt in plain disregard of his anatomy,
then settled before he could tell her to stop it. "In any
case, the electricity didn't go off. Just the lights."

"How do you know that?"

"Because the elevator was still moving when it got
dark. That's how I ended up taking a nosedive. I
thought I was on the ground floor when it stopped."

"You probably pushed the button with the '1' on it
instead of the one with the 'G.' Maybe this will help
you remember that the first floor over here doesn't
mean the same thing as it does in the States." In Europe as well as most of the rest of the world, the first
floor was really the first floor up from the ground floor.
Tanner was surprised that a woman who traveled as
much as Abby would forget that.

There was a clear note of irritation in her voice

when she replied. "I *know* the difference, Tanner. I'm positive I pushed the right button."

The lights came on before he could point out that she shouldn't have gone any farther than just outside of the elevator in the first place. When Abby didn't appear to be in any hurry to get up, he said, "We should probably make a choice here about whether we're going upstairs or down."

She cocked her head as though listening, and Tanner could tell by the increasing noise coming from the lounge that people were probably gathering.

She said, "I don't think I'm in the mood to listen to any where-were-you-when-the-lights-went-out stories."

"If you're still thirsty, I could always go down and fetch our drinks. There are a couple of chairs in my room that look like they might be a tad bit more comfortable than this floor."

"Mine, too, but I was thinking more along the lines of a nice bath."

"That settles it, then. Let's get you upstairs."

She made as if to get off his lap, then looked up at him when he held her firmly in place. "I *can* walk, Tanner. In fact, I should probably try it before my muscles freeze up."

"You can walk in your room," he said. When she didn't try to get up again, he knew she'd gotten the "don't argue with me" message he'd sent her. Reaching for the candle, he blew it out and put it next to the wall. Her handbag was a bit farther along, but he managed to grab it and toss it into her lap without any fuss. Then he got his arms under her in all the right places so that he could stand up without dropping her. He managed, and would have done so even if she hadn't

locked her arms around his neck. But he didn't tell her
her precautions were unnecessary because he liked the
way her breasts rubbed against him when she was that
close.

He liked it so much that he walked all the way up to
the fifth floor instead of taking the elevator. Out of the
corner of his eye, he saw Rory come around a corner to
follow.

When they got to her room, he put her down, unlocked the door with the key she took from her bag,
then watched her carefully to make sure she was walking a straight line as she went inside.

"I'll go down for the drinks. Don't get into the tub
until I get back," he said just loud enough for Rory to
hear. He wanted to talk with his cousin before he went
to bed.

"Thanks, Tanner, but I really don't want anything
to drink now."

"I do. Don't worry, lass. I'll be back before you get
the tub half full."

"I don't recall inviting you to join me." She looked
up at him suspiciously.

He shrugged. "Amnesia. You must have bumped
your head on the way down the stairs."

She lifted a hand to her temple, and winced when
her fingers landed on a sore spot. Tanner closed the
distance between them and put his arms around her
before she could back away. He brushed his lips very,
very lightly over the same spot on her forehead.
"Sorry, bad joke. Is it very sore?"

"I'm not sure. Do that again." She arched against
him to bring her forehead back into contact with his
lips, then sighed and leaned back into the curve of his
arm. "You're good, Tanner, but I still think I'm going

to end up with a very bad headache tonight. Sorry about that."

"If you mean you're sorry we're not going to spend the night making love, don't worry about it. My heart can't take any more jolts today, not at my age."

The look on her face was half-amused, half-mystified. "I know there are a lot of things I'm *appallingly* uninformed about, but I never knew that sex could be so . . . hazardous, even to a man of your advanced years."

"As you say, there's a lot you don't know. Now then, lass, I'm going downstairs to retrieve my drink. I'll be back in a couple of minutes, so don't even think about getting into that bathtub before I come back. I'm not going to jump in with you, but neither am I going to let a woman who has just tumbled down a flight of stairs take a chance of passing out in all that water."

She tried to keep her disappointment from showing. "Don't be melodramatic, Tanner. It was only half a flight."

Tanner paused at the top of the stairs as Rory separated himself from the shadows and joined him. To avoid the chance that Abby might overhear, they went down a full flight before speaking.

"Is she all right?" Rory asked.

"Mmm. She took a tumble in the dark, but got lucky. I imagine she'll be a bit stiff tomorrow, but that's all. Any news on what happened to the lights?"

"Management figures someone overloaded a socket and blew the whole lot out. They got it back on just before I went looking for you."

"The elevator was still working, so not all the circuits were out."

"They must have an automatic backup on that system." Rory lowered his voice and said, "There's nothing that points to this being anything more than what they claim."

"Then explain to me why Abby got off the elevator at the first floor and thought she was all the way down." Tanner felt his cousin's gaze on him and turned to meet it. "She's too well traveled not to have pushed the correct button for the ground level. And since there was no one in the cage with her, we have to assume someone set her up."

"You think she was meant to fall down those stairs?"

"I think it's possible. If I'm overreacting, blame it on a complete lack of information." He checked his watch as they came into the wide central hall. "After I get Abby tucked in, I'll call Wyatt. He should have something by now."

They turned into the lounge and ordered drinks while standing at the far end of the bar. Rory kept his voice low as he spoke. "I agree that we have to assume Abby's in danger. We can't afford to do otherwise."

Tanner signed for the drinks, and they carried them back toward the stairs, silently agreeing that the less time Abby was alone, the better. On the way up, they sorted out the details of keeping an eye on her, which amounted to Tanner taking the night shift and informing Rory when he went back to his own room in the morning. Rory didn't ask why Tanner expected to be able to keep an eye on Abby all night, and Tanner didn't fill him in.

Reaching the top floor, they walked along the hall

to her door where Tanner paused and put his ear to the wood. The sound of her soft humming reassured him, and they went on to his room and stood just inside.

Rory said, "It would be helpful to know what Abby has done to Yoshimoto."

"You didn't find any hint in her room?" Tanner asked.

"The only thing I discovered was that she's got an appointment tomorrow at a big woolen mill out the other side of Killarney. There's a plaid fisherman's hat tucked into the back of a drawer, so I imagine that's what she's after." He gave Tanner the address and phone number of the manufacturer.

Tanner grinned. "I should have gotten you to do my spying years ago. This is almost too easy."

Rory gave him a strange look. "For a minute this evening, I thought you were doing your own dirty work anyway."

"What do you mean?" Tanner looked at him carefully, but didn't see anything beyond the bland expression Rory typically fronted.

"I saw someone come out of her room earlier. Thought it was you until I got close enough to see they were wearing a uniform."

"Probably someone turning down the bed or delivering something."

"That's what I decided. When I searched her room myself a few minutes later, it hadn't been ransacked, and there was a sealed envelope on the table with her name on it."

"Did you open it?"

Rory shook his head. "I didn't happen to have the kettle with me. Next time, I'll come better prepared."

◆————————◆

When Tanner finally returned, Abby had changed into her crimson robe and was sitting on the edge of the tub as she watched it fill with steaming hot water. He offered her one of the two brandies he carried, but she turned it down in favor of the glass of sparkling water she'd already poured. As she turned off the taps, she heard a heavy thump just outside the bathroom door. She went to find Tanner settling into the chair he'd dragged across the room—out of sight of the bath but not so far away that they would have to yell in order to have a conversation.

He sipped his brandy, then told her to get started with her bath because she only had thirty minutes and the clock was already ticking. Abby couldn't think of a single reason not to get on with it. Dropping her robe to the tile floor, she settled into the larger-than-necessary bath with her foot braced against the shower fixture and tried to pay attention as Tanner gave a brief account of what he'd learned downstairs about the mysterious light failure. He went on to tell her about his breakfast with Ms. Browning, eliciting at intervals a response from her that she figured was his way of keeping track of whether her head was above or below water.

So she mumbled when he paused, not listening so much as feeling. Tanner's low, rumbly voice was as soothing as the water, washing over her in a caress so gentle and welcome, she wondered if she'd ever be able to bathe without hearing echoes of the past.

The consequences he'd promised weren't realities, not yet.

When her time was up, his command to get out was

firm, but not enough so as to make her move. She stayed right where she was, wallowing in the luxurious sensation of being looked after by a man she'd wanted close for so very, very long.

He didn't ask her to get out a second time, just came into the bathroom and stood beside the tub with a huge towel in his hands. He didn't say anything until she'd stood up and let him wrap her in the warmth of the towel and his arms.

"You're making this harder on me than is strictly fair," he said.

She leaned into him and sighed. "Don't talk to me about fair, Tanner. You're the one who's gone noble all of a sudden."

He chuckled, and the warmth of his breath at her temple sent chills down her spine. "You're already stiff and sore, Abby. I'm not going to add to it by making love to you in your condition."

"Afraid I won't be able to tell the good hurts from the others?"

"Something like that." With a badly smothered groan, he stepped back and rubbed the towel briskly over her body. The effect of his almost clinical ministrations was nearly sexless, yet there was a gentleness in his touch that she responded to with a slow warming in the vicinity of her heart.

When he'd finished, he plucked her nightgown from the back of the door and put her into it. It was a modest flannel affair complete with long sleeves and a slightly scooped neckline that served the purpose it was intended for: To keep her warm. It also must have served to bolster Tanner's good intentions, because he looked a whole lot less tense when he tucked her into bed a few minutes later.

Abby was up to her chin in down-filled duvet with her arms trapped beneath it when he sat down on the bed and bent over to kiss her. His lips were firm against hers, and she'd hardly gotten accustomed to the idea that he was kissing her when it was over.

He lifted his head a few inches and gave her a grim sort of smile. "I've got some things to do in my room, but I'll be back after that. You go ahead and sleep. I won't wake you when I come in."

"What are you coming back for?" Her tongue slid across her lips in search of his taste as her muzzy brain tried to make sense of why he would return when he'd already said he wouldn't make love to her that night.

"Because sleeping together is just one of those things lovers do."

Abby fought the tentacles of sleep that reached out for her. "If you stay, I'll probably want you to kiss me again." She ruined that statement by yawning, the kind of yawn that showed off her back molars. Not quite polite, but with her hands stuck under the duvet, there was nothing she could do about it. By the time she got her mouth shut again, Tanner had picked up her key from the dresser and turned off the lights. Without another word, he went out, testing the handle behind him to make sure it had locked.

She supposed she only imagined the sound of his fading footsteps as the thick carpet absorbed the reality.

Abby yawned again and snuggled deeper into the covers. She hoped he wouldn't be too long because the idea of sleeping next to Tanner was a strangely comforting one—strange because all previous images of lying in bed with him had been much too arousing for comfort.

Abby fell asleep within minutes, and it was in a dream that Tanner slid in beside her and folded her into his warm embrace.

NINE

Abby was hot, intensely so, burning with a fever that seared her body and fired her soul. The heat rippled through her with every stroke of Tanner's hands across her sweat-slickened flesh, the friction of his callused palms urging her through the door from fantasy to fact.

Abby didn't question how she knew, when he covered her breast with his mouth and began to suckle, that this wasn't a dream. She didn't have the strength for questions or their answers either, needing everything that she had inside her to keep up the wild, passionate pace he set. His lovemaking was a hundred times more vital than she remembered, a thousand times more exciting than her dreams. He touched her where she hurt from wanting him, stoked her excitement with whispered hungers, and caressed her heart with his gentle care.

Her gown had disappeared with the duvet, but she missed neither because she was too hot, too focused on the throbbing need between her legs. Tanner stroked her there, circling the nub within the slick folds with his thumb as he tested her sheath with first one finger, then two.

Heat flowed through her like a circling river, her hands fisting into the sheet when his tongue tracked a slow, wet path from her navel downward. When he blew gently into the curls that clung damply to his fingers, she made a soft keening sound that seemed to originate somewhere deep inside herself.

Tanner looked up, nodded his approval of her abandonment, then bent his head again and took her into his mouth.

The fire burst within her, exploding from her center and flaring outward. She knew she cried out again because Tanner's hand was suddenly there to cover her lips. But he didn't stop what he was doing to her, the suckling, the stroking, the caresses that pushed her higher, hotter.

The explosion came again, fierce and strong, before Tanner slid back up her body to take her into his arms. Her fingers trembled as she stroked his muscle-corded shoulders, and she arched against him until her breasts were crushed into his chest. Dazed, not comprehending anything but knowing there was more, there *had* to be more, she felt him take a deep breath before rising over her to push her legs open wider. They shared the shudder that rippled through him as he began to penetrate her.

The fire burned more brightly now, glowing between them with a ferocity that didn't diminish as her eyelids drifted closed. Tanner filled her with a slow, wondrous heat, beads of sweat dripping from his forehead onto her face as he carefully, unrelentingly pushed into her deepest self. She spread herself wider, then wrapped her legs around his hips because it brought him deeper.

It never hurt, not even the moment when she noticed a slight hesitation on his part, then pressure as he eased past the proof of virginity. All she felt was pleasure in the way he'd awakened her senses and kept them aflame with his possession. He caressed her damp body with his hands as he began to thrust and withdraw, devouring her mouth with wet, hungry kisses as his hard chest teased the painful tips of her breasts.

He filled the night with wonder, her body with fire, and her soul with joy. It was no dream that Tanner had finally come to her, no fantasy that conjured up sweat-slickened bodies and erotic whispers to fill the night air. It was her life, and his, and they were mating in a way that had been postponed years too long.

The blaze within leapt into full conflagration almost before Abby was ready for it and long past the point when she thought she could have withstood another moment. His shoulder smothered her cries, and she felt more than heard the victory of his own release as he threw back his head and thrust into her one final time. Moments later, he collapsed onto her, then rolled to his side, his chest heaving as he held her close. Abby's descent was slower, just as complete but seeming less final, as the muscles in her sheath gently convulsed in the aftermath of their lovemaking.

From the very first moment since she'd stood high atop Grianan of Aileach and watched Tanner approach, she fully understood just what kind of chance she'd taken in letting him inside her defenses.

She'd risked it all . . . and even now, there was no telling if she'd won or lost.

——◆————————◆——

It was light when Abby awoke to find Tanner propped next to her on one elbow, pushing tendrils of hair from her forehead. She blinked sleepily, then smiled when she realized his thigh rested familiarly between hers beneath the covers.

"So that's how lovers sleep together, is it?" she said.

"Only in an ideal world." He bent his head and kissed her with lingering thoroughness, his tongue caressing, not teasing, his lips gentle and warm, the palm of one hand resting on her belly. It seemed a long time later when he said, "I hope you don't mind, but there aren't going to be any apologies. When I woke up in the middle of the night with your butt snuggled against my groin and your breasts filling my hands, it seemed like the only logical thing to do."

Her body flushed with the remembered fire. "I wouldn't have said no if you'd awakened me first."

His eyes darkened in flagrant desire. "There *was* no first, lass. I was already aroused, more so when I realized your nipples were hard against my palms and you weren't even awake." His hand skated downward, feathering across the curls that guarded the sensitive area between her legs. With his thigh he urged her legs apart, then drew a single finger through the swollen folds he found there.

"I suppose I might have kissed you awake and told you what I wanted to do, but I couldn't resist touching you here first," he said, nearly taking her breath away as he hooked a knuckle around the nub he'd toyed into erect awareness. "You were already wet for me, Abby. Just like you are now. Wet and slippery and ready for me to take you. I couldn't resist." His voice ended on a hushed whisper, and he didn't seem to expect an answer as he nuzzled aside the duvet and sucked her breast into his mouth.

She couldn't have answered anyway, not then, or moments later when Tanner pushed a single finger inside of her and rotated it slowly as his thumb teased the delicate nub. Desire shot through her, just as strong as before, just as demanding. She threaded the fingers of both hands into his hair, anchoring herself on the thick silk of it as he pushed her upward, driving her into a realm of passion he'd created, she knew, just for her.

She cried out when he withdrew his touch, then sank her fingernails into his shoulders as he spread her legs and pushed into her without giving her the chance to take a breath. Her delicate skin was tender where he filled her, but not so much that she could ignore the throbbing excitement building within her.

Once he was as deep inside as he could be, Tanner forced himself to be gentle, to go slow with this woman who had never until a few hours earlier felt the full length of a man inside of her. It was heaven and hell, this intimacy that had never felt quite so urgent, and he knew he shouldn't be doing this at all because Abby was likely all kinds of sore. But he couldn't not do it. They were part of each other now in ways he'd only fantasized about before, and he couldn't get enough of her.

He was damned sure he wasn't leaving her bed until he'd climaxed in her sweet, welcoming depths one more time.

Still, he knew enough to be careful with her. Fighting for a grip on his raging desire by holding himself very still inside of her, he positioned himself on his elbows above her and captured her gaze. "If there are any apologies to be made, it should be for this. It's too soon for you. If only you hadn't been so wet when I touched you, I might have been able to wait. But now . . ."

"But now you've gone and made me want you all over again, so what is there to apologize for?"

He sucked in a surprised breath as she moved her hips beneath him. It was harder to do this time, but he made himself stay still, using his body to quiet her movements. "I know that last time isn't anything to go by, but it's quite possible for me to be gentle. It will be easier if you don't try to help."

Her eyes went smoky in remembered pleasure. "It *was* wild, wasn't it? I never imagined lovemaking could be like that. Can we do it again?"

Tanner groaned and dropped his head to rest between her small breasts. From there, it only took a slight move to the side before he had her nipple caught between his teeth.

It was Abby's turn to suck in her breath, and she did it again when he tongued the nipple, then opened his mouth over her breast. He laved the sweet roundness with his tongue, keeping his hips absolutely still as he heard her breathing shorten to small, irregular gasps; then he moved to her other breast as his fingers clutched at the curls at her nape.

He should have known he couldn't control it all, but he'd forgotten that Abby was Abby—unpredictable and wonderfully exciting. The way he imprisoned her against the bed should have given him dominance, but it didn't work out that way, not once Abby discovered the muscles gloving his erection.

Tanner had been busy with her breasts, loving them, worshiping their firm, soft curves, taking gentle bites when he discovered she particularly liked the sweet pain. Suddenly, she tightened around him, using muscles she was born with but had never used, teasing him until he thought he'd go mad.

It only took a second or two, then he was moving, thrusting in and out of her with an urgency that balked at nothing. Caution hovered at the edge of his awareness, and Tanner paid enough attention to it to remember that if he couldn't be gentle, he could be fast. Pushing his hand between their bodies, he found the center of her womanly excitement and brought her to a pulsing climax just moments before he found his own.

In the calm that followed, Tanner held Abby close and wondered if she believed now that nothing could ever again be the same.

Tanner had just finished shaving when there was a knock at the door. Pulling it open, he found a very somber Rory on the other side. He stepped aside for Rory to come in, leaving the door slightly ajar in case Abby stirred from her room.

"What's up?" he asked, hoping it wasn't important because getting his thoughts away from Abby and the wondrous night they'd spent together would take an effort he wasn't up for. Besides, Rory had only been on duty for thirty minutes or so, certainly not long enough for anything major to transpire.

As it happened, he was wrong.

Rory reached inside his sport coat and handed him a plain envelope. "The tip of this was sticking out from under Abby's door when I cruised by after you called. I thought it might be useful."

"It must have been put there after I'd gone," Tanner said. "I see you found your kettle," he added as he slipped a single folded sheet from the envelope.

> Walk into darkness
> One false move and fall from grace
> Indecision's gulf

Adrenaline-fueled fury shot through Tanner, and he would have been out the door and halfway to Abby's room had Rory not blocked his way.

His cousin said, "Room service brought her coffee right after I found this. She's fine, if not a bit surprised by your thoughtfulness."

Tanner should have known better than to imagine Rory wouldn't see to the priorities—namely, Abby's safety—before getting around to details such as informing him of events. His initial surge of panic had made him forget, momentarily, his cousin's special background.

Rory nodded toward the piece of paper. "I assume it didn't escape your notice that it was written in the form of a haiku."

"No, it didn't." Retreating to a chair, Tanner reread the Japanese-style poem. "This confirms last night's blackout was no accident."

"Agreed." Rory eased into the chair opposite. "It's either an accident, or we've got an opportunist in our midst who knows entirely too much about your woman for my peace of mind. At a guess, though, I'd say it was planned."

Tanner agreed. "Too bad Wyatt came up with a blank on Yoshimoto. I'd feel a lot better knowing more about the enemy." The fact that Wyatt hadn't been able to find a trace of Yoshimoto in the Rim's business network was disturbing for the mere lack of information. Either Yoshimoto was so well covered that his tracks were invisible, or he didn't come from the Pacific Rim at all—in which case he was, possibly, more lethal for being anonymous. Wyatt was duly suspicious of the whole setup and would continue to look into it. In the meantime, Tanner knew he was dealing with a man who was likely much more dangerous than he appeared in Phoenix circles. The fact that the Marshall brothers were evading his assistant's queries deepened his concern.

He put that worry aside for the moment and asked, "Do you have anything to add to what we knew last night?"

"Just that the fuse box is inside a wardrobe next to the manager's office. Apparently, they often neglect to lock the door." Rory made a face, showing what he thought of the hotel's security measures, then went over to the table and helped himself to the coffee Tanner had ordered earlier.

Tanner agreed with Rory's logic, but couldn't help looking for holes. He would have felt much better to find one big enough to indicate Abby wasn't in the kind of danger that involved serious threats. "If the fuse box is so handy, why did it take so long to fix it last night?"

Cup in hand, Rory shrugged. "You've been away from Ireland too long, cousin. Those lovely circuit breakers you have in the States aren't nearly as popular over here. From what I saw a few minutes ago when I got a peek at it, this hotel still relies on the old-fashioned fuses—you know, the kind with the round tumblers and lengths of wire that you have to wrap around."

"I thought you said last night that the fuse had been switched off."

"That was their story at the time. This morning, I managed to convince a bellboy to give me the whole tale. According to him, the set of fuses for lights and a few other things had been pulled out and thrown on the floor. Some of the fragile wires were damaged in the process, and they had to rewind them."

Tanner looked at the curt message one more time, then put it back into the envelope. "Assuming this 'accident' was rigged for Abby, how did they know she would be the next one using the elevator?"

"They took a chance, but not much of one. There can't be more than a couple dozen guests in the hotel, and most of them were either at dinner or in the lounge." He finished his coffee and put it aside. "The only thing I can't figure is how they kept the elevator on her floor with the first floor button already set. I'm sure Abby will have an answer when we ask her."

"We're not asking." Tanner tucked the envelope inside his suitcase.

"We're not?"

"No." He snagged his tie from the back of a chair and went to the mirror to put it on. "She's in trouble all right, but until and unless she asks for help, she won't take any—no matter how convincingly we offer it up."

"Interesting approach," Rory said after a pause. "Just how long do you intend waiting for her to come around?"

"Not long." He turned from the mirror and gave Rory a steady look. "When she trusts me completely, she'll tell me. I'm working on that part now."

"And in the meantime . . . ?" Rory let the question hang unfinished.

"In the meantime, we watch her back. Just because she won't ask for help doesn't mean she's not going to get any."

Abby checked her room door to make certain it was locked, then turned and plowed straight into Tanner. His strong, familiar hands curled around her arms as she bounced backward, holding her upright without offending the previous day's bruises.

She looked up at him, screening a sudden shyness behind her lashes. It was difficult, this morning after a night spent in his arms. Torn between the need to be held and reassured and the suspicion that a more sophisticated approach might be expected, she aimed her greeting for something neutral.

"You'd think with a gallon of coffee inside me, I'd be more alert to obstacles."

Amusement flickered across his expression, then something that resembled regret as he dropped his hands to his sides. It was almost as though he'd been waiting for a signal from her that it was all right to touch as lovers touch, to share a restrained kiss and remember the wilder moments just hours earlier. Abby sighed, making a silent note that if she wanted Tanner to react to the vulnerable side of herself, she would have to show it to him.

"It's the carpet, lass. It's thick enough to allow even someone my size to sneak up on people."

"Good thing too," she said, rubbing a bruise on her forearm through the off-white Aran-knit sweater she wore over matching wool slacks. "If the carpet on those stairs had been threadbare, I'd be sporting casts instead of bruises."

He cupped her chin with gentle fingers that evoked breathless memories of the night's loving. The heated look in his eyes told her that he, too, was remembering. "Is that all that's sore?"

"No, but it's all I can decently rub." With a laugh at his outraged stare, she headed down the hall.

Tanner fell into step beside her. "So what's on the agenda today?"

As if you didn't know, she thought, and would have said it aloud if he hadn't begun to steer her toward the elevator.

"Nuh-uh," she said, veering off toward the staircase. "I had enough of that contraption last night."

"I could have sworn it was the stairs that were at fault."

"The stairs were innocent bystanders. It was the elevator that tricked me. By the way, thanks for the coffee," she said over her shoulder. "I'd still be half-dressed and comatose without it."

"I like the half-dressed part."

"You would."

He caught up with her on the first landing and hauled her with tender insistence into his arms. Then he kissed her, so thoroughly and deeply that when he lifted his head, they were both breathing heavily. It had taken only a moment, but in that slice of time he'd succeeded in making her forget there was a world that revolved totally apart from the one within his arms.

"Good morning, love." His voice was husky, deeper than it had been just seconds earlier.

She realized she was standing on her toes with her hands wrapped around his neck, and had no memory of doing either. "I like how you say that," she murmured. "Can you do it again?"

"Later," he promised as he untangled them until they were side by side and heading downward. "For now, let's get some breakfast. I've got a feeling I'm going to need it."

TEN

It was business as usual at the woolen mill where Tanner ordered enough hats to warm the heads of a whole lot of fishermen—not to mention every hunter, golfer, and flea market cruiser in the Pacific Northwest. He may even have bought too many, but that was the price he had to pay if he wanted an exclusive agreement with the mill.

In other words, he'd bought lots to exclude Abby from any chance at a deal. She understood, and hoped he could get rid of the extras in a sale. Quarter-price would clear the warehouse even if it did upset the accountants.

She stood silently watching the transaction, trying very hard to keep a look of pique on her face to cover the laughter that was bubbling inside. She ended up having to bite the insides of her cheeks.

Tanner was so sure he'd gotten her on this one, she thought, so confident, in fact, that he'd invited her along to the factory—without telling her where they were headed, of course—then going so far as to let her drive. She assumed that was because his own car had taken on the characteristics of a shoe: Too tight in the first place and impossible to fit now that the foot was swollen.

She didn't know precisely where he was swollen, and had the discretion not to ask.

They'd taken their time with the brilliant Irish morning, stopping at Muckross Abbey to wander past tombs of various Irish chieftans and noted poets. Lunch was a simple meal of bread, cheese, and draft Guinness at a pub crowded with locals whose accents made the language as foreign as Greek or Russian.

They turned up at the factory without Tanner bothering to explain how he'd learned about the hats in the first place. She didn't ask either. It was part of their game, disregarding the means in favor of adding up the score. Traditionally, methods were more or less straightforward, leaning toward room searches and the like. It had never ceased to amaze Abby how willing telephone operators, bellboys, and waiters were to provide Tanner with the clues he needed to keep up with or ahead of her.

There had also been a period of twelve or fourteen months when he'd been so successful in beating her to the goods that she'd been forced to look for the spy within. She'd found the scoundrel disguised as a weekend clerk who was, in his real life, married to one of Tanner's accountants. When she'd voiced her objections, Tanner had been crass enough to remind her of the apprentice buyer—Tanner's—whom she'd subsidized in exchange for similar information. The apprentice was now working for Abby, just as the accountant's husband had found a job with Tanner.

Everything was fair, she mused, including the room

search Tanner had accomplished in order to ace her out of the hats. A pity she'd had to go to the trouble of setting them up as a red herring, Abby decided as she studied the samples more closely. She would have much preferred that he come in empty-handed at the end of the day.

Until the woman in Tralee called to say she was ready to sign an exclusive contract to supply Desert Reef with her linen separates—ladies' mix-and-match clothing—Abby had to do everything in her power to keep the entire project mum. If she was successful, the separates, hand sewn from the finest linen, would form the basis for her fall line. If she wasn't, then Abby's last shopping expedition would end up a dismal failure that would linger in her mind long after she sold up and moved out.

Tanner shook hands with the owner and turned to find Abby twirling a hat on her finger.

"I could have used one of these last month in Scotland," she said lightly. "If nothing else, my head would have been warm."

Tanner's heart skipped a beat as an alarm sounded deep in his psyche. "Last month?"

She shot him a wry grimace. "Yes, Tanner. Last month. Do you have any idea how cold it can get in Scotland in October? I think if that dog hadn't found me when he did, I would have frozen clear through."

Tossing the hat on the pile, she shivered visibly and led the way out into the sunshine. It took until they were in the car and she was steering it back in the direction of Killarney before he had enough control over his surprise to follow up on her horrifying revelation.

"It's not that I in any way doubt you, but are you positive it was Samuels?" he asked.

"Of course it was Samuels. I saw him following me several times that afternoon. That ugly leather jacket he usually wears is hard to miss." She glanced at Tanner, an incredulous look on her face. "You can't seriously believe someone else let the air out of my tires?"

"It's just that I didn't know it only happened last month. There are some things about this that don't make sense."

"What things?"

He shook his head and tried to sound a whole lot less concerned than he was. "What about Thailand? When were you there?"

"Late summer. It must have been toward the end of August because I remember coming home to a three-day weekend—Labor Day, I expect." She cut through a roundabout without seeming to notice traffic shooting through from the three o'clock position, then geared up to take advantage of the resulting gap in traffic as the less intrepid cars behind her sorted out the remaining slots among themselves.

"Were those the only times Samuels bothered you?"

"So far as I know."

Before she could ask again why he wanted to know, Tanner pressed for more information. "What about Yoshimoto? When did he first make an offer for the boutique?"

"Oh gosh, I don't know." She ran her fingers through her hair before returning her hand to the gearshift. "July or August, I think. It wouldn't have been any earlier because I don't remember even meeting him until that Fourth of July bash the chamber of

commerce sponsored." She slowed for a school crossing and crawled along with impressive caution until
they were clear of it, then put some speed back into
things.

She shot him another sideways glance. "You tricked
me, Tanner. I wasn't going to tell you anything about
Yoshimoto."

"You haven't said anywhere near enough for my
peace of mind."

She didn't respond to his deliberately provocative
statement, but he could tell by the way she crunched
down through the gears as she came up behind a slow-
moving bus that she was bothered.

The tension building in Tanner had nothing to do
with Abby's rambunctious style of driving. She zigged
when a more timid driver would have zagged, took corners at a dangerous cant, and zoomed ahead of more
powerful cars when it became clear they were more
concerned about their paint jobs than getting to a destination in the least time possible. She didn't scare him,
though, because there was a certain flair in her skillful
maneuvering that inspired confidence.

There was also the advantage that anyone following
would have a hell of a time keeping up. Tanner con-
soled himself with that small ray of hope as he kicked
himself for not making the connection between Samuels and Yoshimoto sooner. He had no doubt that there
was one, even though the facts were still scarce on the
ground.

For the most part, though, he acknowledged that
he was still operating on instinct. The coincidence that
Yoshimoto had offered for Desert Reef about the same
time Samuels had begun harassing Abby was a small
one—so small that he wouldn't have made a connec-

tion between them at all if he hadn't just realized one very important thing: The incidents with Samuels in Thailand and Scotland had happened *after* he'd fired the man, not before as he'd assumed.

If Samuels wasn't hassling Abby with merchandise as the incentive, his behavior took on an infinitely more sinister aspect. There were only a few remaining explanations—none of them attractive. The one that made sense coincided with Sandra Harringdon's departure from the bidding. Yoshimoto wanted Desert Reef, and he wasn't taking no for an answer. Samuels was apparently one of the tools he'd employed to ensure the outcome.

Tanner was just beginning to realize how much danger Abby had landed herself in.

She downshifted to take her place behind a Land Rover that was one of several cars strung out behind a slow-moving hedge mower. "What's going on, Tanner? Why all the questions?"

Tanner thought about not telling her, but, in the end, he couldn't do that. It was her own penchant for secrecy that had kept him from seeing the full scope of the danger in the first place. Before he said anything, though, he needed to organize a thicker safety net.

"Take that turn for the Gap of Dunloe. We'll talk when we get there."

She took the turn, then argued about it. "It's just a few hours before dark, Tanner. You're sure you want to do more sight-seeing?"

"We're not going back to the hotel until I know exactly what's going on between you and Yoshimoto."

"And what if I still don't see any reason to tell you anything?"

"That was all right before you started falling down stairs, Abby. Things have changed."

"What things?"

"I fired Samuels last spring, before you ever went to Thailand or Scotland." He met her startled gaze as she took her eyes momentarily from the road. "His expense accounts had begun costing me more than the merchandise he brought back. It had nothing whatsoever to do with you."

"Then why did he—?" She stopped abruptly and took a deep breath before continuing. Tanner checked her for visible signs of panic, but her hands were steady on the wheel and she was paying normal attention to the position of the car within the erratic traffic pattern.

"I don't know why," he said. "I've just put the dates into perspective myself."

"If you don't know that, then how do you make the leap from Samuels to Yoshimoto? I haven't seen either in weeks."

"Unless you've got reason to believe Samuels has a private vendetta against you, then we have to come up with an explanation for his behavior. Barring any other enemies you've neglected to mention, it makes sense to connect Yoshimoto to all this."

"He's not an enemy, Tanner," she said heatedly. "Yoshimoto is just a man who thinks he can frighten me into giving him what he wants. He wouldn't know how to put threats into action."

"You're saying you weren't scared at what Samuels did to you?"

She opened her mouth to argue, but all she said was, "I think you're letting your imagination run away with you."

"You don't know everything I know." If she did, she'd be a lot more worried than she was.

"Then tell me, Tanner. Tell me—"

He cut her off. "We'll talk at the Gap. For now, I've got some catching up to do." He reached into the backseat for the phone he'd taken from his rental car and dialed the number for the hotel. When he asked for Rory O'Neill, Abby made the connection so quickly that she nearly rear-ended the Citroën directly ahead of her.

She didn't, though, and Tanner spent the seconds before Rory came on the line admiring her reflexes.

Tanner waited until they'd reached the parking lot at the entrance to the Gap of Dunloe before speaking. As they sat in the car in the nearly deserted lot, he told her everything he knew, then took the note Rory had found under her door from a pocket beneath his sweater and gave it to her.

He waited in silence as she read it. When she'd gone over it not once but several times, he pulled it from her trembling grasp and put it away.

Her eyes were wide and clear when she met his gaze, and if there was any fear to be seen in them, it was secondary to the brimming curiosity. "Who is Rory?"

"My cousin," he said, lifting a hand to stroke the downy softness of her cheek. "He has experience in matters like this. I called him when I realized something might be wrong."

"But I met him that first morning at Rathmullan. How could you have known? Nothing had happened yet."

"Nothing and everything. You'd hinted Yoshimoto was threatening you, and I remembered the rumors about him and the Marshall brothers. It was enough, I felt, to organize a few precautions." He leaned over the console and brushed his lips across the bridge of her nose, then eased back against the door. The handle dug a hole in his back, but it was the only way he could sit and keep an eye on anyone entering the lot.

Just because Abby drove like a banshee didn't ensure they hadn't been followed.

"Where is he now?" she asked. "I haven't seen him since that morning at Rathmullan House."

"I would imagine that right now, he's on the phone to Phoenix. You heard me ask him to follow up on those inquiries I'd begun."

"But when did he get to Killarney? I haven't laid eyes on him here."

"You have, but you just don't know it." He reached past her and pushed her door open. "Let's go take a ride, Abby. Some fresh air will do us both wonders."

"I want to talk some more."

"We will." He got out of the car and waited until she'd locked it before guiding her up the slope to where a half-dozen heavyset horses lazed in the late-afternoon sunshine. There were as many traps—two-wheeled carts with padded seats—scattered around the muddy enclosure, and the men who drove them stood smoking hand-rolled cigarettes as they waited for customers. One of the older ones broke away from the circle and within minutes, Tanner and Abby were seated across from each other as the pony and trap headed up a narrow, rutted track into the Gap of Dunloe—a knifelike slash cut perpendicular to a range of hills the Irish liked to refer to as mountains.

Their guide was thorough, pointing out the barrack
ruins where English soldiers protecting the first tourists had been quartered, a lake so deep that it was
thought to be bottomless, and the exact spot where St.
Patrick killed the last snake in Ireland. Abby oohed and
aahed in the appropriate lulls, but not even the spectacular scenery could take her mind far from the terse
phone conversation between Tanner and Rory O'Neill.

Even hearing only one side of the dialogue, she'd
known by the time they reached the parking lot that
there was a lot going on that she'd been completely
oblivious to. It frightened her—as much, she supposed,
because she hadn't known as because of the actual
events.

At first, it had seemed unreal—Tanner's almost immediate suspicions that were based on rumors she'd
never heard. His attempts to research Yoshimoto
through a man across the world in Singapore had
seemed equally fantastic. But when she added up the
timing of Samuels's attacks to the previous night's fall,
the pieces formed a picture that was terrifying in its
implications.

> Walk into darkness
> One false move and fall from grace
> Indecision's gulf

Her skin crawled at the realization that there was
another note in her room that was probably a warning
she wouldn't have understood even if she'd read it.

It never occurred to Abby to be angry that Tanner
had gone ahead and organized his cousin to watch over
her without telling her. Had she heard the scandalous
rumors going around Phoenix about Yoshimoto, she

might have jumped to the same kinds of conclusions. As it was, she had something more important on her mind than any petty resentment over the steps Tanner had taken to look after her.

When she'd told Yoshimoto that she was selling Desert Reef to Tanner, she'd put the man she loved in danger. She gave a small gasp, and knew without looking away from the rugged mountain she was pretending to study that Tanner had heard. He reached across the trap and gave her hand a small squeeze. She squeezed back, and knew that she had two things to tell him now.

She loved him. There was no doubt inside of her about it, just as there was no reason to believe it was a recent occurrence. Abby knew without thinking too hard about it that she'd loved Tanner for a long time now. It explained so much about herself, about why she'd never been able to let him far from her thoughts.

She wasn't in any hurry to tell him, though. That could come later . . . that night, perhaps, when they were alone. Certainly by the following morning she should have managed to find the appropriate moment to bring it up. A slow smile creased her face, and she wondered how it was that she knew he'd be as delighted to learn she loved him as she'd been to realize it.

She wondered, then put the thought aside because it wasn't important *how* she knew. She *knew*, and that was all that mattered. The pony plodded slowly up the trail, dragging the trap behind it, and Abby spent the time trying to figure out how to tell him about the other thing she thought he should know.

For his own part, Tanner didn't look any more engrossed in the tour than she was. He was, she noticed, much too busy watching the trail behind them, paying particular attention to the handful of cars that squeezed past them on a swifter ascent to the Gap. Just what he thought anyone would attempt was beyond her imagination, and she couldn't very well ask him—not with the guide standing between them and chattering about the rich history of the Gap of Dunloe.

When the guide suggested they give the pony a rest before turning back, Tanner was quick to agree. Jumping down from the trap, he helped Abby to the ground, then pulled her up the side of a hill toward a point where the guide had indicated the view was worth climbing for. Tall, wet grass wrapped around her ankles, but Tanner's firm grip kept her from sliding backward. He didn't stop until they were hidden from pony and trap by a rocky knoll and the entire Gap of Dunloe was a single panoramic vista.

Abby stared blindly across the valley that fanned out from the base of the Gap and leaned into Tanner as he wrapped his arms around her from behind. "If I'd known what a mess this was going to turn out to be," she said, "I would have never invited you here. I'm so sorry, Tanner. It's just that I never imagined Yoshimoto was serious."

"You didn't have any reason to," he said, giving her a hug for comfort. "It was only by chance that I heard those rumors in the first place. Without that, I probably would have handled things much as you have."

"Except you wouldn't have dragged me into it."

He touched his lips to her forehead. "I doubt if Yoshimoto even knows I'm here. If he does, he'll probably assume we're having another shopping competition. It's not exactly a secret back in Phoenix that we tend to go after the same merchandise."

"Oh, he knows you're here all right," she grumbled, and turned within the circle of his arms until they were facing each other. She lifted a shaking hand to stroke his chin, then threaded her fingers into his hair that lifted and fell in the slight breeze. In the thick knit sweater and wool plaid scarf that draped around his neck, he looked as though he truly belonged in this wild, gentle country of his birth. With his broad shoulders and muscled body, she imagined him as a warrior from another century . . . and prayed she was right, because if even a portion of what he said about Yoshimoto was true, then she'd dropped him into more trouble than most men faced in a lifetime.

She took a deep breath and said, "I told him you were buying Desert Reef."

"You did what?"

"I told him you were buying the boutique. It was all I could think of that would put him off so that Sandra wouldn't be afraid to reopen negotiations. I knew he'd never dare threaten you." She was almost in tears from an interminable hour of dwelling on the terrible thing she'd done, and it took several seconds before she realized that instead of being furious, he was actually grinning.

Her gaze narrowed on him suspiciously. "What's so funny?"

"Not funny so much as astonishing," he said. "I'm in total awe of the faith you have in me. I don't suppose it occurred to you that I might run the same way Sandra did."

She had the grace to blush. "My thinking didn't get that far. Actually, I just assumed Yoshimoto wouldn't take on a man of your reputation."

"And just what is this reputation? I'm dying to

hear." He linked his hands behind her waist so that she stood intimately between his spread legs. "Is this anything like the assumptions you made about my sex life?"

"Actually, it has more to do with the way you handled that street gang last spring. Rumor had it that they threatened to victimize your employees unless you paid them not to."

He was surprised she'd heard about that. It had been, for the most part, a small incident that had been over almost before it had begun. "It was a matter of letting them know how much they themselves stood to lose. Once they understood my position, they were very cooperative."

"Not knowing *how* you did that is what keeps the rumor alive," she said. "In any case, this gets us away from the point. I should never have involved you in my problems with Yoshimoto. Now he'll be after both of us—or Samuels will. Speaking of which, how can you be sure Samuels is part of this?"

"Unless you've made some other enemies that you haven't told me about, it only makes sense that Samuels is working for Yoshimoto. From the way it looks to me, the point is to scare you into selling or make you so tired of being harassed that you do it." He hesitated, then added, "He raised the stakes last night, though, and that worries me."

"Why?"

"Because he must have known you could have broken your neck." He was ready for the shudder that racked her small frame, and used his body to absorb as much of it as she would allow. They stood there for several long moments before he judged her calm enough to discuss the rest. "The thing that worries me is how he thinks he'll get a hold of the boutique if you're dead. I assume your parents would inherit?"

She nodded without looking at him. "They're not business people, though. I imagine Yoshimoto thinks they'll be easier targets."

"If he's figured that much out, then we have to accept just how serious he is." He buried his face in her blond curls and inhaled her special scent that owed nothing to perfume. "It would be helpful to know *why* Yoshimoto wants Desert Reef. Perhaps then we'll have a better idea how to handle him."

"Actually, I've wondered about that from the beginning. It's not like I make an exorbitant profit, although I've done rather well over the years."

He agreed. "If he's looking to get rich, he'd have to set his sights a lot higher."

"Before you told me about the Marshall brothers, I guessed he wanted the boutique as a cover to import something. I was thinking along the lines of antiques, but now . . ."

He took up where her thoughts had trailed off. "It might be drugs, I suppose. With all the stuff you import, it would be easy for Yoshimoto to imagine he could hide a bit here and there."

"Then he's a fool. Customs is a lot more thorough than that."

"As a rule, I'd agree, but what if he already has that base covered?"

"You mean that he might have paid someone off?"

Tanner shrugged. "Theoretically, anything's possible. We're only guessing about the drugs. Since he's not likely to tell us, we'll have to operate under the assumption he's willing to do either or both of us serious harm in order to get his hands on the boutique."

He shot a quick glance skyward and frowned at the fading light. "It's later than I thought. We'd better get back down."

He was about to turn away when she stopped him with a gentle touch on his arm. "Why don't I just let him have Desert Reef, take what he's offering, and get out before someone really gets hurt?"

"Because it's too late for that," he said, and drew her along behind him. "I suspect that once you told him I was involved, he knew he had to move fast to keep us from closing the deal. It looks as though he's decided that the only way to keep that from happening is to get rid of you."

There was a note of wry exasperation in her voice when she said, "Gee, Tanner, thanks for going out of your way to reassure me. I'm sure I'll sleep better knowing all this."

"If you're worried about sleeping, don't be. There are lots of things we can do instead." He began telling her about them in minute detail, and could only imagine her outraged blushes as he led her down the steep incline.

It wasn't until they were nearly at the bottom that he realized things weren't quite as they'd left them. The trap, along with pony and driver, had disappeared. In its place was a dark blue Mercedes sedan with smoky windows that successfully hid the driver from view.

ELEVEN

The incongruity of seeing such a modern machine in the primitive surroundings overwhelmed the rational side of Tanner, which knew that whoever was inside was no threat. Acting from a deep-seated need to protect Abby, he shielded her with his body as the driver's side window silently lowered.

Rory looked out at him and said, "One of the Marshall brothers came through. I thought you'd want to know right away."

Abby peeked around Tanner's broad back and gave an exclamation of surprise. "It's you! I thought there was something fishy about you last night when you wouldn't play UNO with us."

"Fishy?" Rory looked offended.

"Mm-hmm. You said you were tired from driving too far, but the only thing that was wrinkled about you was your suit. Your eyes should have been bloodshot if you were that whipped, but they were perfectly clear."

Tanner quirked an eyebrow in amusement. "I didn't realize she got that close to you."

"Neither did I," Rory muttered.

"The disguise fooled me, though," she said, and there was a placatory tone in her voice that made the men realize she felt the need to reassure Rory. She edged under Tanner's arm and looked down the track. "What happened to the horse?"

"I paid the driver off." His gaze rested on Tanner. "Am I to assume she's not as angry as you imagined?"

Tanner shrugged uncomfortably. "Let's just say she was more concerned about what she did than what I did."

"Excuse me?" Rory didn't even pretend to understand. "Never mind. Get in and you can tell me all about it. We can't turn this around anywhere short of the top, and I'm not looking forward to doing this road in the dark."

Tanner opened the back door and tucked Abby inside before climbing into the front. With Abby leaning over the seat so that she didn't miss a single word, he briefed Rory on Abby's convoluted plot to rid herself of Yoshimoto. When he was done, Rory filled him in on what he'd learned from Tanner's assistant.

"Your man Cummings traced the older brother to Seattle where he's in the process of relocating. After a lot of maneuvering, Cummings managed to get Marshall to tell all." He paused and glanced over his shoulder as though he were uncertain whether to continue.

Abby spoke up immediately. "Don't mind me, Mr. O'Neill—"

"Rory," he corrected her.

"As I was saying, Rory. Don't mind me. I'm only the one who fell down the stairs."

He gave her that point with a brief nod, but they had to wait until he'd negotiated the turnaround before he continued. "Yoshimoto threatened the Marshall children. The brothers were so convinced he was serious that they gave in without a fight."

"Why didn't they go to the police?" Tanner asked.

Rory shrugged. "Losing part of a business made more sense than risking their families. They made a decision to get out altogether, which is why it was so hard to find them. They're starting up again in Seattle."

There were more details, but Abby was no longer listening. Easing back into the rear seat, she tugged at the seat belt and secured it around herself as the men spoke softly in the deepening twilight. Her hands were trembling, and she clasped them in her lap as she thought about the Marshall children and what might have happened if their parents had tried to fight Yoshimoto.

She knew that whatever happened from now on, she would never again take Yoshimoto's threats lightly. That was important, because if she was going to win this battle, she couldn't afford to underestimate her enemy.

Now that she'd brought Tanner into it, Yoshimoto had a weapon against her. She fully understood what the Marshall brothers must have felt when their families were threatened.

She couldn't fault Tanner for trying to protect her when he'd only suspected something was amiss. Now it was her turn to protect him, and she didn't have a clue how she was going to do it.

Only a sliver of light remained in the sky as they reached the parking lot and Abby and Tanner switched cars. Rory followed them back to the hotel—at least, Abby had to assume he was behind her. It was too dark to be sure, and her driving techniques were too ingrained to allow for a shadow.

They reached the hotel more or less together and met in her room for drinks, with Tanner and Abby entering as a couple and Rory making his own way and slipping inside when he was sure no one was paying attention. Tanner opened a bottle of wine he'd bought earlier and poured it into bathroom glasses, and they saluted one another silently before taking a first sip.

It had been agreed in the car that the only way to get rid of the threat Yoshimoto presented was to get rid of Yoshimoto—figuratively speaking, of course. With Rory's contacts at the Irish Garda—police, he translated for Abby—all they had to do was catch him in the act of behaving badly, then let the authorities take over.

Abby let the men know what she thought of that idea. "How are you going to connect Yoshimoto with any of this? If he were here, there might be a chance. But as far as I can see, he's just doing the directing from afar." A thought occurred to her, and she got up and dashed over to the trash can where she'd tossed the unopened note. It wasn't there, and her spirits were sagging as she sat back down beside Tanner. "The maid must have got to it, a shame because Yoshimoto had personally addressed the envelope. The haiku is only typed. We can't prove anything."

Tanner eased back into the deep cushions of the small sofa and rested his arm along the back of it so that his hand lay warm against her neck. "We won't have to. Whoever Yoshimoto hired won't take the fall alone, not if they're given incentives to bring the man on top down with them."

"You think the Irish government would go to the trouble of extraditing him for something like this?" she asked.

Rory spoke up. "I don't think it need get that far. If we can prove the connection through the men doing the actual deed, it will be enough to stop Yoshimoto from bothering you anymore."

Abby rolled a small sip of the heavy red wine on her tongue and shook her head. "That's not good enough."

Tanner flexed his fingers lightly around her neck. "Why not?"

"Because there won't be anything to stop him from doing it again to somebody else." She turned her head sideways to look at him. "Would you rest easy knowing a man like Yoshimoto is out there threatening kids and you hadn't done anything to stop him?"

There was a long silence, then Tanner shrugged with deliberate casualness. "So we don't leave it at that. For now, though, we have to concentrate on setting him up. The rest can come later."

He exchanged a quick look with Rory and had to work hard not to smile at his cousin's similar effort to keep his expression neutral. Abby's insistence that Yoshimoto be removed from a position where he could harm others was something the men had taken for granted without having to speak of it. There were personal kinds of justice that would mete out appropriate punishment when the legal system was too cumbersome to traverse. Abby might not like how they took care of Yoshimoto, but she would have to understand there weren't many viable options.

No one hurt Abby and got away with it.

Rory put his glass down on the table between them

and rested his arms on his thighs. "The main thing we have to do is pinpoint the hired guns."

"Guns?" Abby choked, and Tanner had to slap her back twice before she was breathing normally again.

Rory looked somewhat chagrined. "An expression, Abby. Sorry. What I mean was the man or men Yoshimoto hired. The goons. We need to figure out who they are."

"You might be trained for this kind of skulduggery," she said, "but what makes you think Tanner and I will be of any use?"

Tanner answered for his cousin. "Look at it this way, Abby. We've spent years trying to outthink, outclass, and just plain outmaneuver each other. Rory is merely suggesting we pool the devious skills we've learned along the way and employ them against the goons."

"Looking at it from that perspective, I suppose I should be very good at this."

Tanner edged closer to Abby and slid his arm fully around her shoulders. "First off, I think we can assume Samuels won't be in on this. He's too easily recognizable by both of us."

"You're probably right," Rory said. "But keep your eyes open for him, just in case."

Tanner nodded. "I might have seen one of them at Rathmullan House. I didn't get a good look at him, but now that I think about it, he made an effort to keep me from seeing his face." He went on to tell about the man who'd left his breakfast half eaten.

"So that's one," Rory agreed. "There might be more. Abby, can you tell us anything else about last night when the lights went out? Did you see anyone on your way to the elevator who might have punched the wrong floor?"

Her mouth went dry as she remembered the terrifying plunge into darkness, and she shook her head after replaying the incident in her mind. "There wasn't anyone. I got into the elevator because it was stopped on my floor. I had intended to go down the stairs." She snuggled an inch closer to Tanner and was amazed how much better that made her feel. "At first, the elevator wouldn't go down, and I realized it was because something was stuck in the door."

"What?" both men asked simultaneously.

"A matchbox," she said, then felt the bottom go out of her stomach when she remembered the rest of it. "It was from Rathmullan House."

Rory's reaction was a restrained elevation of a single eyebrow. Tanner's was slightly more vocal, and included words she'd read but never actually heard aloud. For a reason she couldn't fathom, the profanity tickled a funny bone and it was several minutes before she stopped laughing long enough to pay attention. They'd proceeded with the planning without her, and she'd no sooner caught up than Rory excused himself and left.

Tanner glared down at her. "Was that hysterics, or are you having too much fun?"

She tried to look repentant, but knew by Tanner's expression that she'd only met with minimal success. "Sorry, Tanner, but when I woke up this morning, I didn't realize I'd stepped smack into the middle of a B movie. I mean, doesn't this all sound just a little far-fetched to you? Clues smashed in elevator doors, lights that go out in nearly deserted hotels, bad guys skulking in the shadows, and good guys hiding behind fake mustaches?"

"You didn't think it was funny earlier."

"Maybe I quit being scared."

"That would be foolish. Fear will keep you alert. It might even save your life."

She swallowed and didn't have to work at the somber expression that came with his words. "It's not that I'm not afraid, Tanner. But knowing you're with me takes so much of that away. Rory too. I have confidence that between you two, that among the three of us, we can win this." She dropped her gaze to his chin and wondered what he'd do if he knew her fear was for him and not for herself at all. "Just promise me you won't do something stupid and get yourself hurt. I don't think I could bear that."

Life wouldn't be worth living if something happened to take Tanner away from her. She cuddled close against his side because it seemed the only thing to do was hold on tight and never let go.

He must have read her mind, because one moment she was trying to get as close as she could, and the next he was putting his hands around her waist and lifting her onto his lap. Before she could adjust to this new position, he pulled her tight against his chest and held her ear to his heart. "Listen to that, Abby. My heart is beating now, but last night when you fell, it felt as though it stopped. I know my world did, at least for the few minutes between hearing you scream and realizing you weren't hurt."

She felt his warm breath against her forehead, and tilted her head to rest on his shoulder. "I suppose I'm getting rather fond of the way your heart beats when you're around me. There's a lot about the rest of you that I like too."

"Such as?"

"If it's compliments you're looking for, I suppose it wouldn't hurt to tell you that your hair was the second thing that attracted me to you. I love that wild look it gives you." She reached up and caught a handful in her fist, then used it to bring him close enough to brush her lips across his chin. "Samson's strength was in his hair. Maybe that was what really attracted me. Your strength."

"So what was the first thing?" He slid down in the cushion until she was almost lying on top of him. It was a position that suited her—surprised her, too, because there was no shyness at the feel of his erect length pressing against her lower belly.

She let his hair slide from her grip as she feathered kisses in a circle around his lips. "The first thing?" she asked between kisses, chuckling as he tried to catch her mouth and failed.

"That attracted you to me," he reminded her. His hands stroked up and down her back in a way that would have been considered totally innocent were it not for how his thumbs brushed her breasts in passing.

She found his ear with her questing tongue and wondered if he was as sensitive there as he'd taught her she was. Between lush, wet strokes, she thought about telling him that the first thing that had attracted her to him was the way he treated her as a dangerous equal in business. It had been a heady day when she'd realized he didn't just tolerate the presence of her small boutique. He'd seen her immediately as a threat to his own profits and had treated her as such.

In a world that was still dominated by men, it was thrilling to be seen as a peer . . . or, even, a rival.

His hands curved warm and firm around her buttocks, and she decided it wasn't the time to bring up business and her place in that world versus his. It was a time for loving, and she was only beginning to learn in Tanner's arms just how little anything else mattered.

Sucking in a deep breath as his fingers found the side zipper of her wool slacks, Abby left a trail of kisses across his cheek to his mouth, where she began to show him just what love is.

The next morning, they moved to a medium-sized hotel on the outskirts of Cork. The reasons were twofold: First, Rory would be able to see if anyone followed them from the Killarney hotel—although that wasn't strictly necessary as they'd left a forwarding address at the front desk. Yoshimoto's goons had choices, and the last thing Rory wanted was to lose them. The object was to figure out who they were. The second reason for moving was just as practical: By changing to a hotel that didn't rely on tourist trade and was therefore busier in winter, it would be easier for Rory to blend in without being noticed. The fact that the goon/goons would have the same advantage didn't worry Rory. Anyone following Abby or Tanner wouldn't realize they were themselves being watched, and wouldn't guard against it.

They got an early start, leaving right after a quick breakfast. The previous day, Tanner had arranged for his rental car to be collected and Rory had bought a cellular phone so they could keep in touch with him. They were concerned that their departure might go unnoticed in the tomblike atmosphere of the hotel, but that problem sorted itself out in the form of an express delivery for Abby from a certain woman in Tralee. She crowed her delight at receiving a signed agreement for the linen separates, and took the trouble to tell Tanner step by step how she'd set him up.

There wasn't anyone within hearing distance who didn't know Tanner would be paying for dinner that night. As she also managed to name their destination in the same loud voice, the scene was considered a success. On the business side of things, Abby awarded herself two points for outthinking Tanner. It had been one of her more intricate plots, and the fact that it had worked was something she'd remember long after Desert Reef had changed hands.

Even so, they had agreed to take it for granted that they would be followed to Cork. After much heated discussion, it was decided that Abby would drive—the theory being that anyone following would have enough on their plate just keeping up, and therefore wouldn't have time to look in their own rearview mirror.

It worked beautifully. Less than two incident-free hours later, they pulled into the parking lot of the Cork hotel where Tanner had booked him and Abby into a suite. It was an arrangement that suited her perfectly as in only two nights, she'd already grown accustomed to sleeping in his arms. Rory was just down the hall, and without seeming to notice he was behind them, they left their room for an afternoon filled with the kind of activity that Rory and Tanner had agreed was safe and constructive. In other words, they stayed in downtown Cork amidst crowds of students and businessmen, wandering aimlessly past and through shops as though they hadn't a care in the world.

By the time Rory joined them in their suite for a drink, the sun had been down for an hour and Abby's feet were slightly swollen from all the unaccustomed meandering. As Tanner sat on the floor in front of her chair and rubbed her sore toes, Rory reported on the success of their day. Abby tried not to let Rory catch her looking at him, but it fascinated her to note the almost complete physical change he'd effected by curling his hair, changing the wire-rim glasses for tortoiseshell, and deepening his skin color with some self-tanning creme. He'd topped off his disguise with a tiny gold hoop earring, a perfect complement to his new curls.

When she'd called him on the car phone to tell him how nicely the earring suited him, he'd said thank you, and that it was one of a set he'd given his wife for Christmas. Abby had decided then and there that she had to meet a woman who would lend her husband earrings.

Rory ignored her grin and continued his report. "There are two of them, and better at this than I'd expected." He paused to sip his whiskey. "I knew there had to be two, because the first one always seemed to be looking for direction. It took most of the afternoon before I was sure about the identity of the one in charge."

"You're sure two is all?" Tanner asked.

"Hmm. All we have to do now is put Part Two of the plan into action."

"Does it *have* to be Blarney Castle?" Abby asked. "It's such a beautiful old place. I hate the thought of having bad memories associated with it."

"If you do as you're told, you won't see anything of what happens," Tanner said, tweaking her big toe. "It's why we chose it. It's the one place you're familiar enough with that you'll be able to get out of the way without any trouble."

Slouching farther into the chair and shutting her

eyes, she stuck her other foot in his face and waited until he'd begun rubbing that one before replying. "You still haven't told me what you intend to do with these guys."

"We'll let you know when we decide." Tanner squeezed her foot until it cracked, bringing a sigh of bliss from Abby. "Let's go over the part you play. I want to be sure you know—"

She interrupted without opening her eyes. "I walk with you across the grounds into the castle. We climb the main staircase, take our turn at the Blarney Stone—speaking of which, I have absolutely no intention of hanging upside down over a stone five stories above the ground so that I can be endowed with the gift of blarney by kissing it. Is that clear?"

She continued even though no one bothered to reply. "Anyway, after we get past the stone, we go back toward the tower stairs, where, by this time, Rory will have signaled you from the parking lot to let you know if they're waiting for us there."

Tanner interrupted. "Rory, are you certain they won't follow us onto the grounds?"

"Positive. There's only one way in or out. They'd be fools to try anything with any number of witnesses wandering around with cameras."

Tanner agreed. He'd only asked the question to reassure Abby. "And you'll call me on the phone once you've spotted them."

Rory nodded, and Abby continued reciting her unexciting role in the adventure. "Tanner will hurry back to assist in rounding up the goons while I take my time exploring the castle. Between that and staring over the battlements at the countryside, I should be able to dawdle for quite a long time."

"What are you supposed to do if Tanner isn't there to meet you at the bottom?" Rory asked.

"I'll hang around the souvenir shop until he shows up. The fact that he isn't there right away should mean you've got both goons in hand."

"Make sure you stay at the souvenir shop at the castle, Abby," Tanner said. "Do not go back to the one at the entrance. I don't want you anywhere near the parking lot."

She opened a single eye and glared at him. "I know how to follow orders, Tanner. Besides, I can assure you that I don't want to get any closer to those guys than absolutely necessary."

He grunted as though he wasn't entirely convinced, then addressed Rory about that night's schedule. All he and Abby had to do was make sure as many people as possible knew they planned on touring Blarney Castle first thing the next morning. That meant asking everyone from waiters to fellow guests for timetables, suggestions on additional sights worth viewing, and anything else they could come up with to keep Blarney Castle in the conversation.

Rory was tasked with keeping an eye on their room while they were at dinner, just in case someone decided to surprise them. No one bothered, though, and after another short conference on the phone after dinner, it was agreed Rory would keep his distance from Tanner and Abby until the goons had fallen into their trap.

In the meantime, there was a very long night still to get through. Abby and Tanner managed, without any great difficulty, to wile away the hours in each other's arms with hardly a thought to the events that had kept them on edge throughout the day.

The only exception was a terse telephone call from

Wyatt Conners, in which he shared his speculation that
Kenji Yoshimoto of Phoenix was probably the same
man who had been thrown out of his family's newspa-
per business in Tokyo. Apparently—and there was very
little information to be had because the family was un-
derstandably closemouthed about their black sheep—
Kenji had been caught taking bribes in exchange for
influencing editorial policy. Added to rumors linking
him to fast women and designer drugs, it was reasonable to assume the Yoshimoto threatening Abby was
one in the same. Shed of family ties, he'd moved from
passive corruption into aggressively illegal activities.

Wyatt suggested a couple of scenarios for removing
Yoshimoto without bothering the authorities, and Tanner's only regret upon hanging up the phone was that
Yoshimoto's thugs were as close as they were going to
get to the man.

For the time being, anyway. Later, when they returned to the States and confronted Yoshimoto with
the evidence of his conspiracy, there was a possibility
that at least one of Wyatt's suggestions would prove
useful.

In the meantime, there was Abby. Warm, loving
Abby, who fit into his arms and his life with an ease
he'd never dreamed possible. She gave him everything
he hadn't known he wanted from a woman, then took
from him with a passion and happiness that was as irre-
pressible as it was contagious.

When they made love, she gave herself to him with
the kind of sweet generosity that reminded him of what
she'd said that afternoon atop Grianan of Aileach.
*"Surrender is what happens between a man and a woman
who no longer feel the need for defenses between them."*

Tanner kissed the sleep from her eyes and felt love

surge through him as she moved deeper into his embrace. Her silky calf slid across his hip, leaving the satin flesh of her thighs open to his touch. As he began to prepare her for his penetration, he silently admitted that until Abby, his knowledge of what happens between lovers had been appallingly inaccurate.

Until Abby, he'd never even glimpsed the beauty that was love.

TWELVE

The magnificent square tower at Blarney dated back to the fifteenth century and in its glory had witnessed the triumph and tumult of Irish chieftans, their faithful knights in suits of armor, and ladies embroidering it all for posterity. Nestled within gentle hills and surrounded by tall trees that looked older than the fortress's foundations, it evoked a sense of romance and tradition that had lured Abby back on each visit she'd made to Ireland.

She followed Tanner along the narrow walkway beneath the battlements, fuming over her attack of nerves which had thus far prevented her from enjoying even a fraction of the romance of Blarney. It wasn't that anything had happened to make her hands less steady than normal or cause her breaths to come irregularly. On the contrary, she and Tanner had strolled unmolested across the extensive lawns, just two of a dozen or so late-season tourists who saw no reason to hurry beneath yet another brilliant Irish sun.

They'd carefully avoided becoming cornered in any

of the small rooms leading off the tower stairs, going straight to the top to stand in line for their turn at kissing the Blarney Stone. Tanner didn't kid her when she stood by her decision not to hang headfirst over the edge, but handed her everything from his pockets before doing so himself. She used some of the coins to tip the man who was there to make sure Tanner and other intrepid souls didn't lose their grip and make a disgusting mess on the courtyard below. The man's help was more for demonstration than assistance as there was a net strategically placed just beneath the famous stone, but Abby had never allowed that bit of rope to persuade her to try her luck.

"It's not that I'm afraid of heights in general," she told Tanner as they walked along the flagstones back toward the tower. "I can look over the battlements to the ground and not feel a thing."

"I think you just figure you've got enough blarney in you already," he said, and she didn't miss the searching gaze he threw around the open-air tower.

"It probably has something to do with being upside down all this way up." She shivered, wishing they could talk about the goons instead of this nonsense of having to pretend in case someone who counted was close enough to listen. There was, Rory had explained, always the off chance that the goons would follow them into the castle.

She'd feel heaps better if she only knew where Rory was and if the goons had actually showed up. As it was, the distance from the hotel to the castle had been too short for Rory to discover if anyone was following. And as they hadn't spoken with him since just before entering the parking lot, they were ignorant as to what was happening. The only thing they knew for certain was that the goons weren't up on the top of Blarney Castle with them.

They were leaning on the battlements and pretending to be looking at the ruins of an eighteenth-century mansion on adjoining grounds when the phone in Tanner's pocket chimed almost inaudibly. He spoke briefly, then tucked the phone into Abby's purse before anyone noticed it.

His gaze met Abby's, and there was a smile in his eyes that was part anticipatory and part cruel—an aspect of Tanner she'd never seen before. She supposed she should be grateful that he was prepared to do whatever necessary to make things right, but the knowledge that it was her dilemma that had released that primitively brutal quality in him was disturbing.

"They're both waiting out in the parking lot, lass. It will all be over in just a few minutes."

"You still haven't told me what Rory intends to do with them once you catch them," she said, avoiding the infinitely harder subject of the danger he was going into, and just how did he expect her heart to continue beating when she was so very frightened for him?

"You don't want to know," he said, then bent his head and kissed her, his mouth taking hers in an act of possession that she recognized because she kissed him back in exactly the same way.

When he lifted his head and touched her chin with the knuckles of one hand, she knew better than to argue further. Rory was waiting, and there was no more time. "I'll call when the coast is clear," he said.

"Make sure you don't forget."

They paused in front of the tower stairs to let another couple squeeze past, and Abby took her cue to separate. "Let's go down that other way," she suggested loudly, pointing to another section they'd not explored.

"Are you sure it goes all the way down?"

"If it doesn't, we'll just come back up and start all over again."

Tanner pretended to consider, then shook his head. "You go ahead, Abby. I'm too tall to be crawling all over this place. I'll meet you downstairs." He turned and ducked his head as he began the long spiral downward.

Abby watched until he'd disappeared, then squared her shoulders and reminded herself that if she couldn't help, then the least she could do was avoid disintegrating into a mass of nerves while she waited. She followed the narrow staircase downward, not stopping in any of the small, stone-lined rooms even though at any other time, she would have spent hours imagining what they'd resembled in an era long past. Today, though, she had no patience for such romantic meanderings.

Today, Tanner and Rory were fighting a battle—*her battle!*—and the only way she could help was to stay out of sight. Rory had been almost brutal in his insistence she not take a part in the action, dwelling on her lack of training when the observation that she was a very small female didn't overly impress her. In the end, she'd had to admit he was right, that her presence might distract Rory and Tanner from the job they needed to do.

If it hadn't made so much sense, she never would have stood for it.

Exiting a small chamber, Abby found herself on the main stairwell behind a group of tourists who chattered in something that sounded like Danish but could have been Croatian for all she cared. For the moment, her thoughts were divided into two distinct categories: The parking lot and getting outside where the sun could soak the chill of fear from her bones.

The stairs spilled out onto a small flagstone terrace with the souvenir stand along one side. Remembering her instructions, Abby stayed in that area, buying a couple of postcards to keep the shop girl from thinking she was loitering with the intention of stealing something.

Ten minutes passed, by which time Abby had given up all pretense that she was anything but a nervous wreck. She paced up and down in front of the souvenir stand, ignoring the worried looks from the woman behind it as a sprinkling of tourists passed her going both ways.

She checked her watch and was digging in her purse to see if perhaps the telephone had been switched off when it rang in her hand. She snapped it to her ear in total disregard of the earring that dug into her neck. "Well?"

Tanner's voice was easy and strong. "It's fine, Abby. All over. You can relax now."

She knew she wouldn't do anything of the sort until she was in Tanner's arms again, but didn't argue the point. "I'm coming out," she said.

"Why don't you wait a bit," he suggested, and there was an insistence in his tone that she couldn't miss. "Rory is waiting for a friend to come help him take Yoshimoto's goons away. I'd rather you stayed away until they're gone."

Before she could reply, he said, "I'll come find you in a few minutes. 'Bye."

As far as final arguments went, Tanner's disconnect was convincing. Lowering the phone from her ear, Abby took her first deep, unfrightened breath in what seemed an eternity, and only then realized that the woman behind the souvenir stand was staring at her. Unwilling to be scrutinized any longer, she hurried away, taking the path for the Rock Close instead of the other which led to the parking lot. She told herself she wasn't so much following Tanner's orders as she was taking the time to pull herself together before seeing him.

She walked quickly, then paused within the first shadows of the giant yews that towered overhead. Her feet moved more slowly then, her mind finding a kind of peace inside the Close whose massive rock formations and great boulders had formed the heart of a druidic settlement or place of worship. She passed the Witch's Face on her left, but didn't stop. Her destination was a short distance beyond there, the Wishing Steps. As one legend had it, the Wishing Steps had to be traversed downward and upward with eyes closed to have one's wish come true. She'd read in another guidebook that the deed needed to be done walking backward, as well, but had decided long ago that the journey was sufficiently harrowing with closed eyes.

The steps were built into a narrow passageway that tunneled about thirty feet through solid rock, the lower end opening toward the stream. She arrived at the top end and looked around the Rock Close to discover she was on her own—something that would have been impossible at the height of summer. Abby was relieved, because traversing the steps with one's eyes closed was an awkward affair which spectators only made worse. At least this one time she could make her wish and concentrate on it as she braved the uneven steps.

Her wish was so simple that she wasted no time beginning her journey. Closing her eyes, she braced her hands on either side of the sloping wall and felt for the first step. When she was certain that her foot was stable, she moved her other to join it, then slid her hands forward and down. Then she did it all over again, taking each step separately and without any urgency.

The walls became jagged under her fingers, not smooth as they had been at the beginning. The steps were shorter, too, enough so that she couldn't afford to take a single movement for granted. The walls angled farther apart until she could no longer touch both and had to resort to feeling her way on one side only.

Since she'd forgotten to count her steps, she didn't know she'd reached the bottom until the ground leveled out beneath her feet. It was phenomenally difficult not to open her eyes then, and she flashed back to the first time she'd attempted the Wishing Steps. She'd had to start over three separate times, and that was just getting down. Going back up, she'd opened her eyes just a fraction—enough, though, to wipe away any good luck or wishes that she'd earned. As it had been during tourist season and there was a line of people waiting their chance, she'd pretended it hadn't happened and had continued up, finishing with the kind of flair that could only have come from knowing exactly where she was.

She was halfway back up the stairs and able to touch both sides of the passage when an eerie chill settled at the base of her spine. She shivered, then felt a wave of uneasiness wash through her that was unlike anything she'd ever felt before.

Abby was frightened, but not in the way she was when she imagined falling headfirst from the battlements of Blarney Castle. This was different, worse, she thought, because she didn't know what caused it.

She put another foot forward, determinedly keeping her eyes closed as her common sense—always so reliable in the past—told her there was nothing to be frightened of, not unless one were suddenly scared of the druidic ghosts that were rumored to haunt the Close.

She took another step, her palms scraping the rock walls as she pushed too hard against them. It was startlingly quiet inside the passage, more so now that she'd gone from being happy to be alone to the other end of the scale where summer's hordes would be welcome.

She faltered as her foot came down on a small pebble, but it wasn't that slight misstep that made her give up before her goal had been reached. Rather, it was the faint hiss of a guarded breath that put her senses on full alert and made her open her eyes in time to see a man standing over her, his arms reaching out for her, his expression unreadable in the dim light.

For a moment, she thought it was Tanner coming for her, then Yoshimoto lunged forward, not reaching for her as her mind had originally assumed but pushing. *He was going to push her down the steps!* There was nowhere to run, no time to think, no chance to scream as she flung herself at his feet in a desperate attempt to unbalance him, to save herself.

Her shoulder cracked into his shins and suddenly he was falling, flying over her head, his foot knocking her on the chin as his own forward momentum toppled him head over heels and down, down the narrow, uneven steps, the only noise the sound of his body meeting solid rock, again and again, until it was over and all she could see was the shadow of a man sprawled beneath her.

Echoes of death pounded in her ears, a stunning moment of absolute quiet in which the ghosts of another era came to claim one of their own. And then it was silent no more, as Abby began to scream and scream and scream. . . .

THIRTEEN

In the days that followed, Tanner and Abby didn't talk much about what had happened. At least, not to each other. It was enough that they had to go over it again and again with the authorities, for whom no detail was too small or insignificant. Rory's presence—or, rather, his *participation* in events—assured that they were spared the indignity of doubt and suspicion. It was simply a matter of professional courtesy, Tanner had explained to Abby without telling her why Rory merited this special treatment.

She didn't care why. It was enough that they didn't put her under the bright lights and accuse her of murdering Yoshimoto—a ridiculous enough scenario as she *knew* it wasn't her fault he was dead. Yoshimoto had tried to kill her, not the other way around.

Arguments for self-defense aside, there was still a body in the local morgue and she was grateful not to have to be made to feel guilty about it. It was bad enough that she felt guilty about *not* feeling guilty.

Somehow, though, she couldn't summon up much of any feeling for Yoshimoto.

Except anger. It made her absolutely furious that he had been so ready to end her life over nothing more than a business transaction.

"How *dare* he presume to put a value on my life," Abby fumed, pacing from the windows to the bed and back again.

Tanner sat sprawled in the chair he'd dropped into ten minutes earlier when they'd returned from their last visit to the Garda Station, his feet crossed at the ankle and stuck out far enough that she had to go around them or over. She did both, over on the leg toward the window, around as she returned to the bed.

He hoped she didn't forget one time and trip over him. After two days filled with interminable interviews with a wide variety of authorities—American and Irish —he doubted he could move fast enough to catch her.

Two days, and it was finally over. It could have been worse, he knew. Thanks to Rory, the last details—including depositions regarding Yoshimoto's hired goons —had been finished that afternoon and they were free to leave Cork. Before heading out, Rory had invited them up to Ballycastle to meet his wife, Kate, and Abby and Tanner had been happy to accept. Tanner told his cousin they'd be there in a couple of days, that they wanted to take their time and see a bit of the country-side. It had been a long time since he'd taken a leisurely look at his native country.

On the practical side, he hoped that by the time they reached Northern Ireland, Abby might have chan-neled her intense anger into something more useful. For now, though, he was content that she'd avoided the more common by-products associated with violent death. She had no nightmares replaying the scene, no compulsion to dissect everything that had happened, no bouts of irrational fear that she wasn't or would never again be safe. She didn't cry or tremble or any of those things people sometimes did when the tension of unfamiliar situations became too overwhelming.

Two days earlier when he and Rory had found her crouched at the top of the Wishing Steps and screaming her head off, he wouldn't have believed that she would soon be recalling the scene with anger rather than fear. Tanner supposed he should have expected something like this from a woman as unpredictable as Abby. Rory certainly hadn't been surprised. He'd pointed out that anger was about the healthiest reaction she could have, and was consistent with her strong, aggressive character.

Tanner watched her mad pacing from behind half-lowered eyelids and knew he'd better try to cool her down before she exploded. "If you don't change your route, you're going to do serious damage to the rug."

She accommodated by switching to walk around his feet on the window-ward leg and step across on the way back. "It makes me *crazy* that he paid someone to try to kill me."

"Actually, he only paid them to hurt you. He saved the killing part for himself."

"I *could* have been killed when I fell down the hotel stairs," she muttered, hugging her arms to her chest in such a way that her yellow sweater was drawn taut across her breasts.

"You're just mad because the contract was on the cheap side. Don't let that bother you, Abby. The price of the job probably equates with the degree of difficulty, not with the value of the target."

Her eyebrows quirked with the first hint of humor he'd seen all afternoon. "I hope you're not suggesting I'm easy?"

"Nothing with you is ever easy, Abby," he murmured. "Yoshimoto will probably spend all eternity regretting he didn't know that about you."

"If he'd taken no for an answer, none of this would have happened in the first place. Stupid, *stupid* man."

Tanner's gaze had dropped to a point that was level with her breasts, so he could only imagine the red flame of anger in her cheeks. He didn't spend too much energy worrying about her anger, though, not when there were other, more distracting things on his mind. Things like the way her nipples pushed against the soft fabric of her sweater, their outline so clear because she wore nothing more than a thin camisole against her skin. He thought about the bit of satin and lace that was hidden behind the almost demure sweater, the scrap of modesty that matched the daringly brief panties beneath her calf-length wool skirt.

He thought about it, and wondered how it would feel to suckle her through the satin, how Abby would arch against him as the slick fabric caressed her firm curves. Would she react as strongly as she had the night before, when he'd stripped her naked and rubbed against her wearing faded denim jeans and his favorite cashmere pullover?

Tanner felt the strong, insistent swelling in his groin as he recalled her wild, almost frantic abandon as he'd pinned her with his body against the wall and made love to her where they stood. It had happened almost without warning, Tanner thinking that after a rugged day with the police, Abby would dive for the tub the moment they reached their suite. He'd been prepared to wait until she relaxed, until the hot water had drained the day's trials from her body before he touched her with the purpose of igniting another kind of tension.

Instead, she'd kissed him the moment he closed the door, a wet, openmouthed kiss that had eclipsed his good intentions and drawn him into the whirlwind of her passion.

There was a shift in the environment, and Tanner realized that Abby's pace had slowed to a speed that was less frantic, less possessed than before. His gaze dropped to the bottom of her skirt that swirled just below the tops of her soft leather boots, and he couldn't help smiling as he remembered early that morning when she'd been dressing.

They'd been in a hurry, late because they'd made love once too many times and their ride to the Garda Station was waiting. He'd imagined himself in a torture chamber or worse, being in the same room with Abby in various stages of dress, watching without being able to touch, knowing it would be hours before he could do anything about the hardness behind his zipper.

First she'd paraded between the bathroom and bedroom in camisole and panties, and if he'd thought that was bad, she'd pulled on thigh-high stockings . . . then nothing more for the eight minutes and twenty-one seconds it took to curl her hair and put on her makeup.

Salvation, he'd imagined, had come when she pulled on the yellow sweater and skirt. The boots themselves were harmless enough—low-heeled and clinging to her calf all the way up to her knee.

He'd been rendered nearly paralytic, though, as he'd watched her struggling with the tight-fitting boots, her fingers hooked into loops at either side as she pulled and tugged, her skirt billowing to flash glimpses of thigh above her stockings. She'd finally gotten control of the skirt; she tucked it up around her hips so that Tanner hadn't had to content himself with flashes. He could see all the way to the point where her panties skimmed between her thighs, hiding her secrets but showing him exactly where they were hidden.

He'd wanted to go on his knees, then and there, to skim his hands up past the leather, across the nylon until the soft, velvety flesh of her thighs was under his hands and the satin panties against his mouth.

He'd been waiting to do that all day. Abby said something, and he said, "Mm-hmm," without losing the image in his mind.

"Tanner, you're not paying attention to me!" She spun to a stop with a foot planted firmly on either side of his legs.

His eyelids were pleasantly heavy as he forced his gaze upward. "How do you figure that, lass?"

"I just said . . ." Abby let the thought go off without finishing, realizing as she caught the heated, wanting expression in Tanner's gaze that whatever she'd been about to say didn't matter. Nothing mattered, except for this thing between them that got stronger with every breath she took.

Then again, this was an opportunity not to be missed.

A smile tickled her mouth as she filled in the blank with words she'd never said to him before. "I just said that I loved you. Somehow, I expected more than 'Mm-hmm' for a response."

Dark eyebrows lifted in a faint show of surprise.

"Give me a break, Abby. It's not like it's the first time you've said it."

"Oh?" Her thoughts bounced against each other as she examined her memories for any hint that he might be right. When she came up blank, she scowled. "I don't remember saying that before."

"It was last night, right after we made love—"

"Which time?" she demanded.

He hesitated a moment as though searching for an elusive fact, then smiled. "I'm not sure, except that we were in bed. You were lying on your stomach, your face buried in the pillow, and I was trying to get you to move over so I could straighten out the sheets." He reached out to snag her hands and began to draw her closer, her legs splitting wider with every step she took. "I distinctly remember hearing you say you loved me just before you said good night."

"How could you hear me if my face was in the pillow?"

"I heard." Tanner held her lightly by the wrists, his thumbs massaging the tender skin there.

Her breath caught in her throat at his gentle caress, which gave away nothing of the passion she saw in his gaze. "And what did you say?"

Tanner bent his head and touched his lips to the inside of her wrist, then looked up at her through dark lashes that couldn't quite conceal the humor in his expression. "I said the same thing."

"Which was?" She needed to hear the words aloud, capture his commitment to her with a pledge neither of them took lightly.

To admit they loved each other was the closure she'd been seeking for three long years.

"Good night."

"Why you—!" The impulse to whack him on the side of the head was stymied by Tanner's hold on her wrists. Before she knew it, he'd jerked her down to straddle his hips as his laughter was muffled by her breasts.

"You're a louse, Tanner Flynn," she protested, then lost interest in even a pretense at pique as he pushed her sweater above her breasts and began sucking a nipple through her thin camisole. Her fingers threaded into his hair and she held on tightly as he used his teeth with delicate precision on the swollen nub before moving across to the other.

"Still think I'm a louse?" he asked as he wet the satin with his tongue and found the excited flesh peaking beneath it.

"Mm-hmm."

His laugh was harsh and short, then he muttered something about women who didn't pay attention and pushed his hands up under her skirt.

Within moments, Abby had no more control over the words coming out of her mouth than she did over her body, which Tanner caressed with such sweet demands. She might have said anything, for all she knew.

She might even have said she loved him.

She must have, because when it was all over and she lay sprawled with languid abandon across him, Tanner said, "I love you, too, lass. I love you, too."

The fire was burning low in the hearth beside them, giving out a steady glow as the evening wore into night. Most of the hotel's guests had moved into the next room for dinner, leaving Tanner and Abby behind to enjoy the resulting quiet. They'd eaten early, sharing a huge steak and baked potatoes delivered by room service before dressing to come downstairs for a brandy and the company of people who knew nothing about the horrible events at Blarney Castle.

There had been nothing in the press about the incident, partly because Abby and Tanner had refused to talk with reporters, but mostly because the authorities had no wish to blight the romantic nature of Blarney Castle—the number one tourist spot in all of Ireland— with adverse publicity. As the death had been that of a foreigner and had nothing to do with Ireland beyond the fact it had happened in that country, there was no need for the local population to know anything.

Even Yoshimoto's family had agreed with the media blackout. There had been no question about Yoshimoto's brother accepting Abby's account of events; he had, in fact, offered apologies on behalf of his family for his brother's dishonorable behavior. At the end of their short meeting, he'd mentioned to Tanner that he intended to pursue the matter of the Marshall brothers to see what could be done to repair whatever damage his brother had incurred.

All in all, everything seemed to be working toward some sort of solution. Everything . . . except what Abby was planning on doing once they left Ireland.

Tanner looked at her over the pile of dominoes they'd just collapsed and said, "Tell me about this travel business you're buying into, Abby. You haven't said anything beyond the fact that you're using the money from Desert Reef as financing."

She grimaced. "With Sandra not answering my calls, I'm beginning to have doubts that the boutique is going to be sold after all."

Abby hadn't spoken to Sandra since she'd called her

from Rathmullan to tell her they wouldn't have to worry about Yoshimoto any longer. Now that they *really* didn't have to worry, Sandra was nowhere to be found.

"That doesn't answer the question." He pushed the dominoes to one side and rested his forearms on the table. "Tell me, Abby. Are you planning on leaving Phoenix?"

"And if I am?"

His stomach clenched, but he maintained a calm expression. "I like Phoenix, but I suppose I could get used to living somewhere else."

"You'd give up Tanner's Rift for me?"

He didn't even have to think about it. "If you asked me to, then yes, I would. Luckily, I don't see that it would be necessary. Cummings already runs it for the most part anyway, since I spend so much time away. We would just make it a more formal arrangement."

"And what would you do to keep busy?"

"Open another store, I suppose." He grinned as the thought took hold. "I've always liked the idea of expanding."

Her gaze drifted down to where he held her hand in his, and when she looked up at him moments later, there was a brightness in her eyes that hadn't been there before.

She said softly, "Then it appears that whatever I decide doesn't matter, does it?"

"Not unless you decide not to marry me." He turned her hand over in his and stroked the third finger where he hoped to soon see his ring. "I think I'd have a problem with that."

"Marriage?" Her hand trembled slightly, and he squeezed it reassuringly.

"Mm-hmm. Have you made up your mind yet?"

"What do you mean, made up my mind? We've never even discussed marriage before."

He grinned. "Sure we did."

"When?" She was beginning to look suspicious.

"A couple of hours ago." He leaned even closer and dropped his voice to a low rasp. "You probably don't remember, lass, because it was right after you opened the zipper on my jeans. I had two fingers deep—"

"Hush!" Her face flamed with embarrassment, but it didn't last because Tanner was laughing and soon she was laughing along with him.

She shook her head in exasperation. "I swear, Tanner, you can't get through even one conversation without reducing it to sex."

"Three years is a long time to wait for it, Abby. It's going to take a while before I can put it back into perspective." He waggled his eyebrows theatrically. "It's a good thing you're so insatiable, lass. We make a good pair."

"Is that why you asked me to marry you? Because we're good in bed?"

"We're *great*, Abby. In bed and on the floor and everywhere else we make love, but that's not why we need to get married."

"Then why?"

"Because we love each other too much to spend our lives with anyone else." He took her other hand and held them both on the table between them, his gaze locked on hers. "It would be a waste to throw that away."

Her eyes seemed to melt into brilliant pools of light and warmth. "Do you really love me that much, Tanner?"

"I really do." His throat was dry from swallowing air that wouldn't seem to go down any other way, and he was certain that if she didn't answer him soon, he'd be sick or would faint. Still, he made himself say it again, just in case one more time would help his plea.

"I really do love you, Abby. I always will."

The fire popped, her face lit up with an absolutely radiant smile, and her voice was honey soft when she said, "Of course I'll marry you, Tanner. Why else do you think I brought you all the way to Ireland?"

Why else indeed? he thought, and closed the space between them until their lips were touching. The kiss, as gentle and promising as a summer's rain, sealed their future with all the love and trust they held in their hearts.

When Tanner finally took Abby back to their suite, he made love to her with a mixture of pride and possession that a man can only feel for a woman he has claimed for his own. And when Abby loved him back, it was as though all the passion and joy in the world was hers to share with him.

They were lovers in the purest sense of the word, defenseless against each other, surrendering all that they were and rejoicing in what they would build together.

FOURTEEN

It didn't take Tanner long to realize that traveling with Abby—as opposed to being behind or ahead of her—was a challenge in its own right. She had a special knack for spotting signposts to obscure sites that were only briefly, if at all, mentioned in the guidebook. He found himself taking abrupt detours down narrow lanes, fording streams by foot when they judged the water too high for the car, and climbing hillsides where sheep grazed with a sublime lack of curiosity. Sometimes the reward for their perseverance was a little visited stone circle. One time, it was a lump in the ground that was—if they were looking at the right lump—the grave of some forgotten warrior felled by another mightier than he.

Tanner learned to be grateful, no matter how insignificant the object of their search, because at least they'd found it. Heaven help him if Abby saw something in the guidebook that proved elusive in the light of day. She wasn't a woman to take defeat lightly, and dragged Tanner through more mucky fields and cow pastures than he cared to remember.

After a particularly wet scramble through a bracken-infested streambed that eventually led to a stone of dubious historical value, Tanner drove straight to the nearest pub and ordered them both coffees with a healthy dose of brandy on the side.

"You're obsessing, Abby," he said, warming his hands over the peat fire.

"Is that a verb?" she asked, glancing up from the guidebook. Her eyes sparkled with mischief beneath still-damp curls, and there was a quirk at the corner of her mouth that was a sure signal she was toying with him.

It astonished Tanner how much he enjoyed being toyed with.

He clung to the illusion that his point was valid. "If it isn't, it should be. Just because something's listed in a book doesn't mean we have to find it."

She looked up from the guidebook in surprise. "You know me better than that, Tanner. If I'm going to provide a unique service in the travel business, I have to see everything for myself."

"I thought you were just buying into a travel agency."

"That would be boring." She tucked the book aside and clasped her hands around the glass of brandy. "Anyone can make airplane or hotel reservations. I plan to put together voyages for the discriminating traveler, not just trips."

"Not everyone is going to care about old rocks and graves."

"But there will be plenty who do," she argued. "I'll put together other packages for Ireland that include more traditional sight-seeing, but so many of those sites are closed during the winter that it would be a waste of time to do now."

Tanner left the fire and eased into the chair next to Abby's. "Do you plan on checking every detail for yourself before putting each tour together?"

"Mm-hmm."

"That's a lot of traveling." They'd already agreed that Phoenix was an excellent place to be in the travel business, but the thought of Abby being gone for long periods was one he hadn't considered. It didn't take any time at all for him to realize he didn't like the idea.

"I won't be gone any more than I am now," she said. Before he could say that was too much, she added, "I was thinking last night that if we planned carefully, you should be able to come along on most of my trips. They would be ideal opportunities for buying."

He cheered up tremendously. "You could even help me shop."

"For a price." A wide grin split her face, and when she lifted the brandy to her lips, Tanner knew he'd been had.

It took three days to work their way north. As she did every morning before they hit the road, Abby called Rory to see if Sandra had been in touch. She'd left his number with Sandra's assistant because she and Tanner were traveling without any idea of where they'd spend each night. Rory wasn't in, so it was Kate who gave Abby the good news.

"Miss Harringdon called last night," Kate said, the Irish lilt in her voice as pleasing to Abby as what she was saying. "I told her we expected you here in Ballycastle tonight, but she said she needed to speak with you as soon as possible. She wasn't terribly pleased that we didn't know where you were staying last night."

Abby felt a prick of annoyance that Sandra was acting impatient when Abby had tried without success to contact her for several days. Then she realized that Sandra might have heard about Yoshimoto and felt it was safe to come out of hiding. She said as much to Kate.

"Still," Kate said, "she seemed quite anxious to speak with you. And as we didn't have your hotel, she said she would try again this morning."

"But it's the middle of the night in Phoenix!"

"As I said, she seemed anxious." There was a pause, then Kate added, "She should be ringing anytime now. Shall I ask her to call you there?"

Abby chewed the inside of her lip, her gaze fixed across the bedroom where Tanner was fastening her suitcase. They'd already breakfasted, and she wanted to get moving before the day's sunshine degenerated into something not quite so pleasant. Sandra could wait until evening. A few hours couldn't possibly make any difference.

"Thanks, Kate, but we're on our way out. Could you please tell Sandra I'll call her tonight? Unless it storms, we plan on spending the afternoon at the Giant's Causeway, then we'll head over to your place."

"When I told her last night you would return her call, she said it would be easier for her to call you, that she didn't know where she would be today. Apparently, she's been moving around."

"Which explains why she's been so hard to get through to. Never mind. Just tell her we're on our way and to call tonight if she can."

"If it rains, I'll expect you early. The causeway is no place to be in a storm. Those cliff paths are treacherous when they're wet."

When Abby put down the phone a moment later, Tanner had everything ready to go. He said, "We could wait and talk with Sandra if you like."

She shook her head. "That's all right. My bargaining position won't be helped if I look too anxious, and I don't want to have to lower the price just to get it over with."

He grinned. "I wouldn't worry about it. Sandra only has to look at what you did to Yoshimoto to know you're a tough cookie."

"What *I* did to him!" She scowled at Tanner. "You're a wicked man, Tanner Flynn."

"Just making a point, lass." He picked up their bags and herded her toward the door. "Compared to what you've been through lately, negotiating with Sandra should be a snap."

Where Blarney Castle was the number one tourist attraction in the Irish Republic, the Giant's Causeway held that title for Northern Ireland. To describe the phenomenon as the result of an eruption of red hot lava from an underground fissure that crystallized some sixty million years ago into the shapes seen today is akin to describing a rainbow as nothing more than light scattered by mist without even mentioning color.

The Giant's Causeway is a geological wonder spread across several kilometers of spectacular cliffs and shores, the main interest lying in the nearly thirty-seven thousand hexagonal basalt columns jutting up from the sea or cut into the face of the cliff. The pathways along the cliffs with their commanding vistas are often bottlenecked with visitors who simply can't tear their eyes from the spectacular scenery.

Situated at the norther tip of the Emerald Isle, it was just about as far from Cork as one could get and still stay on the island . . . which explained why the legendary giant, Finn MacCool, chose that point to build his bridge to the Scottish island of Staffa. Or so the story went.

As Tanner and Abby strolled hand in hand the mile or so down to the main spill of rocks, Tanner recounted the legend he'd learned at his mother's knee, about Finn MacCool and his rival giant over in Scotland named Benandonner. Finn wanted to fight Benandonner and began to build a causeway when he couldn't get a boat strong enough to carry him. Then Finn heard Benandonner was coming to him, and he decided to trick the Scot by dressing as a baby. He instructed his wife to tell Benandonner that Finn was her child and he should see the father. One look at the baby and Benandonner was off, smashing most of the Causeway in his haste to get back to Scotland.

When Tanner added that there were similar rock formations on Staffa, Abby was inclined to take the legend as fact and dismiss the scientific explanation as nonsense.

"It's much easier to believe in giants than to swallow the fact that these columns are sixty million years old," she said. They were standing at the bottom of a particularly spectacular collection of columns known since Victorian times as The Organ. "These are so uniform that I find it difficult to accept they're an accident of nature."

"You'd rather believe Finn MacCool was as precise as he was ambitious?" Tanner asked.

"Yes, I would." Abby looked up to meet Tanner's laughing eyes and found her breath caught by the sheer contentment she saw there.

"Then let's walk up that path," he said, pointing to a narrow trail cut into the side of the cliff. "The view is not to be missed."

Abby considered the waning light. "Are you sure we have time? It's getting late. Nearly everyone is gone already." She counted no more than a dozen people wandering atop the stubs of columns along the shore. Not that there had been many tourists around earlier, but even most of those intrepid souls had headed back to their warm lodgings.

She raised the zipper of her coat another inch, chilled despite the sunlight that sliced across the horizon. It was full up winter in this part of Northern Ireland, and they were just lucky it wasn't blowing a gale force wind or pouring down rain.

"We won't go all the way to the end," Tanner said, "and there's a cutoff halfway back where we can climb to the top of the cliff and return to the visitor's center that way. Unless you're cold?" he asked, nudging the zipper on his own jacket closer to his chin.

"I imagine the hike will keep us warm." Her gaze swept the length of the path that was visible from where they stood, and she noticed a long, steep section where it cut up to the cliff top. "Or should I say climb?"

The wind gusted, and Tanner lifted a hand to brush the hair from his eyes. "It's just a short climb, lass, but worth it. I'll show you the Giant's Eye. It's so big, you'll wonder how such an enormous man was capable of such delicate work."

"If it's that big, maybe the part about masquerading as a baby wasn't a fable after all," she said, and led the way because there wasn't room for both.

A helicopter rounded the headland then and went right past them, the chop-chop cut of its blades a strange counterpoint amidst the almost primitive setting. They decided it was probably a routine army patrol, keeping an eye on the coast for anything from smugglers to mariners in trouble. The foreign sound of the helicopter had long since faded by the time they came to a switchback, and Abby looked back to discover that with the exception of another couple coming in their direction, they were the only ones on the cliff face.

The path climbed gently upward, drawing them steadily to a level that was halfway up the steep cliff face. Abby noticed the strong-looking barriers that had been constructed at those points where the drop from the path was nearly vertical, and was grateful someone had taken the trouble. She would have been more pleased if they'd put railings all along the path instead of just at the critical spots, but guessed it had been enough of a challenge to haul the materials and build what they had. Still, it unnerved her to think how easily someone could stumble and fall over the edge.

She spoke without looking away from the path. "I think I'm going to recommend that all my clients come here in the middle of winter. Think how crowded this must be in summer."

"A few hundred people crawling all over the place does tend to take away from the Causeway's charm,"

Tanner said. A few minutes later, he caught her arm to pull her to a stop.

"What?"

"The Giant's Eye," he said, pointing at a dark oval shape that appeared to have been pressed into the otherwise red rock.

Abby gave the formation a quick appraisal. "He was a big guy."

"Rather disproportionate, though. I forgot to point out his foot down below. It's five or six feet long—a bit stunted if this eye says anything about his size."

"You sound as though you've spent more than one afternoon climbing around here," Abby said as she turned to look out to sea where the sun dipped low on the horizon.

"Rory's parents have always lived near here," Tanner explained. "Before I moved to Phoenix, we'd come here every time I visited."

Leaning against the hip-high wooden rail, she sighed. "I wish the night would hold back just a little longer. It's so beautiful out here, I don't want to leave."

His back was to the path as he rested an arm across her shoulders. "Five minutes, lass, then we'll have to go."

"Ten?"

"Sorry, but no. I don't want to get caught on that cliff path in the dark."

"Then promise to bring me back someday?"

"Every year." Looking across the ocean that shimmered with light and shadows as the sun dropped lower, Tanner had to agree with Abby. He didn't want to leave either. The Giant's Causeway had always had a special effect on him, and sharing this quiet moment with the woman he loved filled him with the kind of peace that could only come from total contentment.

Hearing footsteps, Tanner glanced over his shoulder to see who was coming. It was the couple that had been following, now no more than twenty feet away. He stifled the surge of resentment their intrusion provoked and was about to look away when the man took his hand out of his pocket and pointed a gun straight at Tanner.

FIFTEEN

Abby felt Tanner's body tense beside her, but it didn't sink in that something was wrong until she saw the grim set of his jaw as he looked down the path. A chill of foreboding curled around her spine, and she followed his gaze to the two people standing about ten feet away.

The dying rays of the sun glinted off the thing the man held in his hand, focusing her attention on it to the exclusion of all else. She knew it was a gun—even though she couldn't recall ever looking at one from this precise angle before—and it was pointed straight at them. At Tanner, actually, but in that split second of comprehension, she got the general idea of what it felt like to be looking down the wrong end of something that had the potential of tearing a hole or two in her goose-bump-covered flesh.

She was absolutely terrified.

Beside her, she could feel the subtle shift of Tanner's body as he slowly dropped his arm from her shoulders and said, "I knew you were greedy. I just didn't figure you were stupid too."

Startled because she realized Tanner had recognized him, Abby lifted her gaze from that ugly blue-black piece of metal to the face of the man holding it. Beneath the Seattle Mariners baseball cap were the regular features of an unremarkable face. It was familiar to Abby but without being able to see the eyes behind the sunglasses, it was not one she immediately recognized.

Then he took off the glasses and waited, almost expectantly, she thought, and she realized she was supposed to know him. She was about to throw up her hands in defeat when it came to her.

"Samuels!" she said, the couldn't stop herself from adding, "I never realized what a nondescript person you really are. I almost didn't recognize you without that horrible jacket. What happened? Did some biker take a fancy to it?"

"Shut up!" he growled, waggling the gun in a manner that was menacing only because she was scared to death he'd accidentally pull the trigger. Intuition told her Samuels was almost as uncomfortable holding the gun as she was facing it—a moot point so long as he kept pointing it in their direction, but something to remember if the dynamics of the situation changed.

It amazed Abby how fear could focus one's thinking. There was no question in her mind that Samuels was there to finish what Yoshimoto had started. She also knew that if she thought about it long enough, she could figure out why he was bothering and how he'd found them. However, the question of survival eclipsed most of her curiosity.

"If you're in this for the money," she said, "I'm

afraid you're going to be disappointed. Yoshimoto won't be writing any more checks."

"He never did." Samuels's laugh was harsh and short, and before she could puzzle that one out, Tanner said, "Look who's standing beside him, Abby."

She shifted her focus to the side and had no trouble at all identifying the woman staring back at her. Although she'd tucked her long red hair beneath a knit watch cap, Sandra Harringdon's distinctive green eyes and classic features were unmistakable at this distance and as familiar to Abby as Samuels's leather coat.

"Sandra?" Abby shook her head in an attempt to sort through the unrelated facts and thoughts and put them into a logical sequence. "What are—?"

"What am I doing here?" Sandra's lips curled into a cruel smirk, and she took a couple of steps forward without getting in Samuels's line of fire. "Surely a smart woman like you can figure that out."

In the few seconds since she'd been interrupted, Abby had figured it out for herself—the essentials, anyway. In any case, she knew enough to realize that of the two, Sandra was infinitely more dangerous than Samuels, with or without a gun. Glancing up at Tanner, it struck her that he was looking at Sandra as a man might regard a snake coiled to strike.

It appeared they were in complete agreement.

"Have you been in on this from the beginning, Sandra," Tanner asked, "or are you just stepping in to pick up the pieces?"

"Does it matter?" she returned, her voice edged with humor as she smiled triumphantly at Tanner.

"Just curious," he said, and it was only then that Abby realized he'd begun to edge between her and Samuels. She couldn't imagine what he expected her to do if he succeeded in shielding her from their view. It wasn't as though she could just sneak down the rugged cliff face and make a run for it.

Tanner continued speaking in a low, inoffensive tone. "It was a few months after Samuels began harassing Abby that Yoshimoto popped up with his offer to buy Desert Reef. I wondered why he waited so long, but I guess you've got the answer to that."

Malicious glee flashed in Sandra's green eyes. "I put Samuels to work as soon as I decided to buy that silly boutique. Yoshimoto was just there for added incentive."

"I can guess how you recruited Samuels. It would have been easy to convince him to do your dirty work once you discovered I'd fired him."

Abby could have sworn she heard the frantic beat of her own heart as Samuels stepped forward until he was even with Sandra. "Everyone knew about your private war with Abby. I was only too willing to help it along."

Tanner stiffened visibly, and with the wind blowing his long hair straight back, away from the strong bones of his face, Abby imagined he resembled his warrior ancestors. "I've already promised myself that I'd deal with you, Samuels," he said. "I suspect that I'm not going to be very civilized when I finally get around to it."

"You talk big for a man with a gun pointed at him."

"And you're shaking a lot for a man holding a gun."

The thrumming of her heart was so loud now that it wouldn't have surprised Abby if everyone could hear it. Then Samuels's eyes darted sideways and Abby turned her head to look as the helicopter they'd seen earlier rounded the spit of land no more than a hundred yards away. She had barely a moment to realize it hadn't been her heart broadcasting its rhythm in Surround Sound before Tanner grabbed her hand and tore off down the path, dragging her in his wake like so much flotsam until her feet got the message and hit the ground running.

She didn't think about how he'd nearly ripped her arm from its socket or the whiplash she'd undoubtedly suffered in their bid for freedom. She tried not to think too much about the gun-toting prankster-turned-gangster who—if she dared to look—was likely hard on their heels as they fled.

There was no way, though, that she could avoid thinking about how close they ran to the cliff's edge, the rim of the world as far as Abby was concerned, sudden death the price of a single misstep. She shied away from the absolute edge to her left and ignored the shouts from behind as Tanner slowed to push her ahead of him, letting go of her hand as the path narrowed.

A missile flew out of the rocky hillside to her right —a ricochet, she imagined, such a pretty word for a bullet gone wild—and she swerved without thinking. That was a mistake because the other side was the one that went more or less straight down. The heel of her foot caught the edge, then went out from under her. Abby's own momentum drove her body past the point of no return. Her arms flailed in the air as Tanner skidded to a stop on the pebbly surface and grabbed the only part of her he could reach. His hand clamped around her ankle, and she instinctively threw her arms across her face as she swung head down to crash against gorse-padded boulders.

From the moment she'd felt the solid bite of his hand around her ankle, Abby had stopped worrying about falling to her death. Now, though, as she hung upside down over a particularly nasty piece of cliff face, it took every bit of control she could muster to keep from screaming her head off.

If this was anything like kissing the stone at Blarney Castle, she didn't want any part of it.

"Tanner?"

"Yeah?"

She thought he sounded a bit winded.

"I don't like this much."

"I didn't imagine you would." She felt his hand curl around her other ankle, and tried not to think about all that empty space between her and the cliff's bottom as he pulled her as carefully as he could back onto the path. She could hear Samuels and Sandra saying stupid things like "Don't drop her" and "I'll shoot if you make a wrong move." She almost said "Excuse me, but I'm not in the mood for this anymore," except that she didn't figure it would get her anywhere.

Moments later, she was standing next to Tanner and assuring him that aside from a couple of scratches on her face and hands—injuries she wouldn't have noticed if he hadn't pointed them out—all that was wrong was they were back where they'd started before the helicopter had done its flyby.

"That was an unnecessary stunt," Sandra said once they'd resumed their former positions. "We don't have any intention of harming either one of you—if, of course, you do exactly what I want."

Sure they wouldn't hurt them, Abby thought, knowing that Sandra wouldn't have told them so much already if she intended to let them walk free. To keep her suspicions from showing, she confronted Samuels. "You should listen to your boss. Don't you realize you damn near killed me with that thing? I suppose I'm lucky your aim is as bad as your taste in clothes."

"I told you once already to shut up!"

Tanner said more or less the same thing under his breath, wishing Abby would let him handle this. Keeping the focus on himself was about the only way he could protect her. He had to try to keep her in the background, do anything that would give her a chance when it came down to the crunch.

They wouldn't get another chance to run, and the only other option was to disarm Samuels. The trickiest part about that would be keeping Abby out of the way of a stray bullet.

He returned his gaze to Sandra as if Samuels wasn't worth worrying about. He knew their only viable prospect of survival was to keep Sandra talking, but time was running out. The night was coming fast, and Sandra was too smart to let herself get caught on the cliffs after dark. Even moving at a fast clip, it would take at least ten minutes to reach the top of the steep, uneven steps. He doubted Sandra was in that good of shape, and could only hope she didn't realize the slim margin that was facing her.

A moment later, that margin was reduced to nil as Tanner saw they were no longer alone. On the trail about fifty feet behind where Samuels and Sandra stood, the hunched-over shape of a man moved silently forward. Careful not to let his focus shift from the couple in the foreground, Tanner raised his hand to the level of Abby's shoulder blades and fisted his hand in the thick wool of her coat.

When Rory made his move, he needed to be sure he had Abby where he wanted her.

Abby must have noticed the new tautness to her

coat because she moved her shoulders in protest. Tanner just tightened his grip and said to Sandra, "I'd be interested in knowing how you managed to get Yoshimoto on your team."

"There was a small matter of an incriminating letter I, well . . . stumbled across regarding his dealings with the Marshall brothers. He was only too willing to play along with me in exchange for my silence on the subject." The light was fading fast, but the scornful sneer on her face was clear. "He was nothing more than a punk with a bank account. I should have known he'd make a mess of things."

"But what was the point?" Abby demanded. "I was perfectly happy to sell Desert Reef to you weeks ago."

"I can't afford what you want for it," she said roughly. "I figured that if I had Samuels and Yoshimoto soften you up, you'd just be glad to get it off your hands." Her scarlet-tipped fingers curled around the lapels of her calf-length raincoat as the wind gusted across the cliff face. "It would have worked, too, if Yoshimoto hadn't decided to take it too far."

"A pity you don't have better control over your people," Abby said with flippant disregard of Samuels's renewed waggling of his gun hand.

Sandra hissed. "It was sheer idiocy for him to think that negotiating with your parents would be easier than convincing you into giving up. Even if they were a walkover, *I don't have the time anymore*! I need Desert Reef *now*!"

"Why?" Abby's question was just as adamant.

"*Because I gave my word I'd have the conduit open by the first of the year, and you're still standing in my way!*" she raged. Her fingers were arched and stiff like claws on an attacking grizzly until she brought herself under control. "You gave me the idea with those silly little emeralds. With all the merchandise you import, it will be a snap to hide a few gems among it. I've already made the contacts, but it's taken all my extra cash to finance my share. Now my partners are threatening to pull out if I don't move the gems soon. Once you've signed the agreement, I plan to register the sale and start shipments immediately."

Tanner thought he was hearing things when Abby's delighted laughter rang out in the clear evening air. He nearly smiled at the almost comical look of outrage in Sandra's expression, but decided against it. It was one thing to keep her talking, and quite another to push her into doing something before Rory was in position . . . which would be anytime now.

Abby stopped laughing long enough to ask, "Just how do you plan to get Desert Reef now, Sandra? I'm hardly likely to sign anything when I know you'll probably shoot me the minute I do. I'm not as stupid as the people you hire are."

Tanner added his own two cents. "If you're getting into details and all, that gun's going to put holes in any accident scenario you might be planning. I'd think twice about this if I were you."

It was Sandra's turn to laugh. "I already have, Tanner. The way I look at it, Abby can either sign the papers I have in my pocket or watch Samuels shoot you. Assuming she goes along with this without you being shot, I'll ensure her silence on the subject of how I obtained her signature—not to mention my little gem-importing sideline—by telling her about the man I've hired to kill you if anything . . . shall we say, legal? . . . happens to me."

Tanner assumed that the sudden hiss of Abby's indrawn breath was a prelude to some speech that would range from "How dare you" to "You won't get away with this." He was wrong.

Abby exhaled long and deep. "Then I guess you're going to have to shoot him, because I won't sign."

"I don't believe you."

"Try me."

Tanner was pretty sure he didn't like the tone of Abby's voice, but was too preoccupied with Rory's approach to do anything about it.

Sandra shot Tanner a malevolent look. "I was under the impression the two of you were involved."

He shrugged. "So was I."

"Then I can only hope you'll convince her to sign or I'll have Samuels shoot the both of you."

He tightened his grip on Abby's coat and said through gritted teeth, "There's only one problem with that, Sandra."

"What?"

"No one hurts Abby and gets away with it."

Except Tanner, and he didn't have any choice, not this time. Hoping it would hurt both of them less than the alternative of being shot, he shoved her to the ground before diving for Sandra. Abby landed on her stomach with a solid whoof, but Sandra let out a shrill scream as Tanner plowed into her and spun her against the cliff wall. He pinned her there with her arms wrenched behind her back as he quickly searched for weapons as Rory relieved a flattened Samuels of his. He didn't find anything except a set of keys and an envelope that he assumed held the papers Abby might have been forced to sign if Rory hadn't shown up when he had.

"You okay, Abby?" he said over his shoulder as he

yanked his belt from the loops of his jeans to wrap around Sandra's wrists.

"Great."

"You're sure?"

"I'm *fine*, Tanner," she said emphatically as she pushed herself onto her knees and surveyed the damage to her palms.

If there was a certain enthusiasm missing from her expression, Tanner imagined it was simply because she hadn't gotten her wind back.

Either that, or she was disappointed that she'd missed the opportunity of watching her lover being plugged with bullets.

He finished securing Sandra's wrists, then shoved one of his aunt's hand-sewn handkerchiefs into her mouth when she dared complain about the rough treatment. He hated the thought that the beautiful linen would be ready for the trash after this, but he'd heard enough out of Sandra to last him a lifetime. Glancing across to where Rory was performing similiar functions on Samuels, he spared a moment to regret he'd not been the one to tackle his former employee.

The temptation to push him over the wooden barrier to smash onto the rock below was strong, one he might not have been able to control. That bullet had come too close to Abby for him to ignore. He said as much to his cousin as Rory dragged Samuels to his feet.

Rory's teeth flashed in the semidarkness as he tucked the pistol into his waistband. "That's why I signaled for you to take the woman. I figured you didn't need that kind of aggravation, not with the wedding and all to worry about."

"Rory, how on earth did you know we were in trouble?" Abby asked.

"The same way these two found out where you were. Kate told Sandra where you were headed when she called, then mentioned it to me when I came home." He pulled a small flashlight from his pocket and handed it to Abby. "I couldn't shake the feeling that something was wrong, and decided to come take a look. If I was wrong, it wouldn't have been a wasted trip. The Giant's Causeway is always worth the stop."

Keeping one hand on the belt at Sandra's wrists, Tanner turned and looked down where Abby still knelt in the dirt. "What do you say, lass? Do I still have a wedding to worry about?"

The moon shone on her face as she lifted her chin in pure defiance. "If you think you can get out of marrying me simply because I didn't turn to jelly when your life was threatened, then you've got another think coming."

He reached down his free hand and pulled her up beside him. "If I hadn't known you'd seen Rory coming, I might be feeling a wee bit insecure now. It's not every man who marries a woman with nerves of steel."

Her grin was quick and wide. "Maybe the next time you'll remember that and not be so eager to shove my face in the dirt."

"I wasn't taking the chance that Samuels would get off a shot."

"And just who is the bigger target, do you think?" She wound a hand around his neck and brought him down to her level. "Next time, Tanner, remember that my life would be nothing without you in it."

"There won't be a next time," he growled, then took the kiss that was waiting on her lips.

Their mouths had hardly touched when she drew back and said, "I would have given her the store and everything in it if she'd so much as touched a hair on your head."

"You'd do that for me?" he murmured.

She didn't even have to think about it. "Only until I knew you were safe. *Then* I'd go after her."

"Oh?" He thrust his fingers into her hair and held her head still, his lips just a breath from hers.

"Mmm." She twined the other arm around his neck and sighed. "No one hurts the man I love and gets away with it."

THE EDITOR'S CORNER

Wrap up your summer in the most romantic way with the four upcoming LOVESWEPTs. Chivalry is alive and well in these love stories, so get ready for the most delicious thrills as each of the heroines finds her knight in shining armor.

Beloved for stories that weave heartbreak and humor into a tapestry of unforgettable romance, Helen Mittermeyer opens this month with **DYNASTY JONES,** LOVESWEPT #754. She is beautiful, spirited, a flame-haired angel whose lips promise heaven, but Aaron Burcell has to discover why his missing racehorse is grazing in Dynasty Jones's pasture! Honeysuckle Farm has been her sanctuary until Aaron breaches the walls that keep her safe from sorrow. Dynasty awakens every passionate impulse Aaron has ever felt, makes him want to slay dragons, but he must make her believe he will not betray her trust. Immerse yourself in this moving and tender tale of a love that heals with sweet and tender fire by the ever-popular Helen Mittermeyer.

Catch **ROGUE FEVER**, LOVESWEPT #755 by Jan Hudson. Long legs in dusty jeans, eyes shaded by a cowboy hat, Ben Favor looks every inch a scoundrel—and Savanna Smith feels his smile as a kiss of fire on her skin! She'd come to the sleepy Mexican town to trace a con man, but her search keeps getting sidetracked by a mesmerizing devil who makes her burn, then fans the flames. Savanna is the kind of woman a man will walk through fire for, but Ben will have to battle charging bulls and bad guys just to call this teasing temptress his. Award-winning Jan Hudson escorts you south of the border where the smart and sassy heroine always gets her man.

No city sizzles like New Orleans in Faye Hughes' **GOTTA HAVE IT**, LOVESWEPT #756. Once he'd been the most notorious jewel thief in the world, stealing from the rich for charity's sake, but now Remy Ballou insists he's gone straight—and Michael Ann O'Donnell fears for the legendary gems she's been hired to protect! His rogue's grin has haunted her dreams, while memories of his caresses still heat her blood. His words make her burn and his touch makes her shiver, but will the pirate who captured her soul long ago bind his heart to hers forever, or vanish in the shadows of the night? Find out in this steamy, sultry love story from Faye Hughes.

Debra Dixon explores the dangerous passions that spark between dusk and dawn in **HOT AS SIN**, LOVESWEPT #757. Emily Quinn is on the run, desperate to disappear before anyone else loses his life to save hers—and Gabe is her only hope! Tempted by her mystery, he agrees to help her evade her pursuers, but hiding a woman whose nightmares draw him into the line of fire awaken yearnings in his own secret heart. Once Gabe becomes more than a safe place to run, Emily strives to show him that forever will not be long enough. Let Debra Dixon lead you through this darkly sensual and exquisitely potent story about risking everything for love.

Happy reading!

With warmest wishes,

Beth de Guzman

Shauna Summers

Beth de Guzman   Shauna Summers

Senior Editor   Associate Editor

P.S. Watch for these spectacular Bantam women's fiction titles coming in September: With **LORD OF THE DRAGON,** Suzanne Robinson, one of the reigning stars of historical romance, presents her latest captivating love story in which a willful beauty and a vengeful knight cross swords; winner of the Catherine Cookson Prize for Fiction, Susanna Kearsley debuts as a spectacular new talent with **MARIANA,** a suspenseful tale of time travel that may be one of the most hauntingly beautiful love stories of the year. See next month's LOVESWEPTs for a preview of these enticing novels. And immediately following this page, look for a preview of the wonderful romances from Bantam that are *available now!*

Don't miss these extraordinary books
by your favorite Bantam authors

On sale in July:

DEFIANT
by Patricia Potter

STARCROSSED
by Susan Krinard

BEFORE I WAKE
by Terry Lawrence

DEFIANT

by "master storyteller"*
Patricia Potter

Only the desire for vengeance had spurred Wade Foster on, until the last of the men who had destroyed his family lay sprawled on the dirt. Now, badly wounded, the rugged outlaw closed his eyes against the pain . . . and awoke to the tender touch of the one woman who could show him how to live—and love—again.

"He'll be all right now, won't he?" her son asked.

Mary Jo nodded. "I think so. At least, I think he'll live. I don't know about that arm."

Jeff frowned. "Do you think he might be a lawman?"

"No," she said gently, "I don't think so."

"He wore his gun tied down."

"A lot of men wear their guns tied down."

"Did he say anything to you?"

She shook her head. She hated lying to her son, but she didn't want to tell him his new acquaintance had so coldly said he'd killed three men.

"Maybe he's a marshal. Or an army scout. He was wearing Indian beads."

"I don't think so, Jeff," she said. "He could just be a drifter."

"Then why did someone shoot him? Did he say?"

She shook her head, telling herself it wasn't a lie.

* *Rendezvous*

Wade Foster hadn't explained exactly why he'd been shot.

"Can I go see him?"

"I think he needs a little privacy right now," Mary Jo said. "But as soon as those biscuits are done, you can take some in and see if he can eat them."

Jeff was scuffing his shoes on the floor, waiting impatiently for the biscuits. She sought a way to expel some of that energy. "Why don't you get some wood for the fireplace?"

He nodded, fetched his oilcloth slicker, and disappeared out the door, eager for some action, even if it was only doing chores. She was hoping there would be a school next year; currently, there weren't enough families to support one, and she'd been teaching him herself from the few books she'd been able to find.

She stirred the broth as she kept her ears open for sounds beyond her bedroom door. Wade Foster should be finished with his personal needs now. He would need a wash and a shave.

She'd occasionally shaved her husband. It was one of the few personal things he'd enjoyed having done for him. But she hesitated to offer that service to the stranger. It had been an intimate thing between her and her husband; they had even occasionally ended in bed, though he usually preferred night for lovemaking. In some ways, he had been prudish about lovemaking, feeling there was a time and place for it, while Mary Jo thought any place or time was right between husband and wife as long as the desire was there.

The thought brought a hot blush to her cheeks and a yearning to her womanly place. It had been nearly three years since she'd last been loved. Hard work had subdued the need but now she felt the rush of heat deep inside.

She shook her head in disgust at herself. She couldn't believe she was having such feelings for the first stranger that came limping along. Especially this stranger.

But she just plain couldn't get Wade Foster out of her mind, not those intense eyes, or that strong, lean body under her bedclothes. Perhaps because of his grief over his son. She'd known grief, but she had never lost a child. And she'd never seen a man so consumed by sorrow.

He was a very disturbing man in many ways and she was foolish to harbor him without checking with the law.

Perhaps when the storm ended, she would ride to town and make inquiries. If she could ford the stream. If—

The door banged open and Jeff plunged back inside, rain flying in with him. Jake stayed outside, barking frantically.

"Men coming, Ma," Jeff said. "A lot of them."

Is anyone after you?

I expect so.

Almost without thinking, she made a decision.

"Jeff, don't say anything about the stranger."

"Why?" It was his favorite question and she always tried to give him answers. This time she didn't know if she could.

She looked at her son, wondering what kind of lesson she was teaching him now. But she had to protect the man they'd rescued. She didn't understand why she felt so strongly about it but there it was.

She tried the truth. "I think he's in trouble but I don't think he's a bad man."

Jeff thought about the answer for a moment. It was *his* stranger after all. He had found him. Well, his dog Jake had found him. And Jake liked him. That made the stranger all right in his book.

He nodded.

Mary Jo hurried toward her bedroom, giving only a brief knock before entering without invitation.

Wade Foster was on the side of the bed, the sheet obviously pulled quickly in front of his privates. His face was drenched in sweat, the color pale, his lips clenched together.

"Men are coming," she voiced aloud. "Could be a posse."

He tried to stand but couldn't. He fell back against the pillow, swearing softly. "I don't want to bring you trouble."

"No one could know you're here. The rain would have erased any tracks," she said. "I'll turn them away."

He stared at her. "Why?"

"I don't know," she said frankly.

"I don't want you or the boy involved."

"We already are, Mr. Foster. Now just stay here and be quiet."

"I don't understand you."

Mary Jo smiled. "Not many people do."

A loud knocking came at the front door, accompanied by Jake's renewed barking. She wished she'd had time to hide Wade Foster, she would just have to make sure no one searched the house. Thank God, everyone in this area knew she was the widow of a Texas Ranger and the heir of another. She would be the last person suspected of harboring a fugitive.

Casting a reassuring look at Jeff, she hurried to

the door, opened it and faced the sheriff and six of her neighbors.

"A man was found dead, killed some four miles to the west," Sheriff Matt Sinclair said. "We're checking all the ranches and farms."

She gave him a warm smile. Since the day that she and Jeff had come to Cimarron Valley, Matt had been kind, attentive, and concerned that she was trying to run a ranch on her own. Others had been contemptuous.

"In this weather?" she asked.

"The dead man appears to be a miner from his clothing, though God only knows what he was doing here." He cleared his throat, then added reluctantly, "He was shot once in the leg and then in the throat at close range. Cold-blooded killing if I've ever seen one. Just wanted to alert everyone, check if they've seen any strangers around."

Mary Jo slowly absorbed the news. Wade Foster had tried to warn her but she hadn't been prepared for the details.

"Do you have any idea who did it?"

"That there's the devil of it," the sheriff replied. "No one's seen or heard anything. Could be just plain robbery, and the killer's long gone, but I want to be sure everyone's warned."

"Thank you," Mary Jo said.

"I don't like leaving a woman and kid alone," he said. "One of my men can stay with you, sleep in the barn."

Mary Jo shook her head. "My husband taught me to shoot as good as any man and I wouldn't be reluctant to do it," she said. "Jeff here is just as good. And Jake would warn us of any trespassers. But I thank you for the offer."

"Well, then, if everything's all right . . ." His voice trailed off.

"Thank you for coming by, Sheriff." Mary Jo knew she should offer them something, particularly coffee but it was too risky. She started to shut the door.

The sheriff added, "I'll send someone over every couple of days to check on you."

"No need."

"Just to make me feel better," he said with a slight smile.

Mary Jo tried to smile back, but couldn't. She felt terribly deceitful.

Tell him, something inside her demanded. Tell him about the murderer in your bed.

But no words came. She merely nodded her thanks. As she watched him and the others mount their horses and ride away, she wondered if she had just made the worst mistake of her life.

"Susan Krinard was born to write romance."
—*Amanda Quick*

STARCROSSED
by Susan Krinard

At sixteen, Lady Ariane Burke-Marchand had loved Rook Galloway with all the passion and pain of unrequited love. It didn't matter that the handsome Kalian was separated from her by birth and caste and mansion walls. All she knew was that this exotic, mysterious creature called to her in ways she couldn't fathom or resist. But that was eight years ago, eight years before the deadly riots that pitted Marchand against Kalian and turned the man she worshiped into an enemy she loathed. . . .

Hudson ducked his head. "Permission to examine your hold and cabins, Lady Ariane. A formality."

A breath of wry laughter escaped her. "I'm not likely to be harboring fugitives on my ship, but I'll clear you."

She led him into the cargo hold and left him there, making her way through the final air lock and into the *d'Artagnan's* living quarters. There was something almost oppressive in the empty silence of the common room; even the cockpit seemed less a sanctuary than a cell.

Ariane shuddered and dropped into the padded

pilot's seat. *Don't think about it*, she commanded herself. *At least this ship is something you can count on. Something certain.*

One by one she ran through the preflight routines: checking the stardrive's balance for sublight flight, priming the ship's life support system, carrying out all the necessary tests. Again and again she forgot sequences that she knew by heart, remembering Rook's face.

Remembering how he had made her feel. . . .

No. Her fingers trembled on the keypad as she made the final entries. *You won't have to think about it much longer. It's over. It's out of your hands.*

But the memories remained while the ready lights came up on the control panel. She leaned back in the pilot's seat and passed her hand over her face.

Honor. All her life she'd been raised by the codes of the Espérancian Elite. Like the *d'Artagnan*, honor was solid and real. It had been insanity to doubt, to question. Duty and honor would send her back to Espérance. Honor would give her the courage to face a life of confinement. To accept.

To forget Rook Galloway.

Letting out a shuddering breath, she rose and began to pace the tiny space of the cockpit restlessly. Hudson should have been done with his "routine" check by now. She flipped on the ship's intercom.

"Mr. Hudson? I'm ready for takeoff." She waited, tapping her fingers against the smooth console. "Mr. Hudson—"

"Here, Lady Ariane."

She whirled, with reflexes honed through years of training as a duelist. Hudson stood just inside the cockpit, a disruptor in his hand.

Aimed at her.

Her first impulse was to laugh. Hudson looked so deadly serious, his mouth set in a grim line that seemed so much at odds with his boyishly untouched face. But she clamped her lips together and balanced lightly on the balls of her feet, waiting.

"Did you find some—irregularity, Mr. Hudson?"

He moved another step closer. And another, until he was within touching distance. "Call for clearance to take off," he said, gesturing with the 'ruptor.

Ariane revised her first assumption. It wasn't what she had supposedly done; Hudson had simply gone crazy.

"I know—how it must be, Mr. Hudson. Alone here, far from home—you want to go back home, is that it? To Liberty?"

He stared at her, light blue eyes shadowed beneath his uniform cap. "Liberty," he repeated.

Considering the best way to move, Ariane tensed her muscles for action. "You must feel trapped here, so far from home. After what we saw . . . I understand. But—"

His smile vanished. "Trapped," he said softly. "What do you know about being trapped, Lady Ariane?" His voice had gone very deep and strange. "Call the tower for clearance. Now."

For the briefest instant Hudson's eyes flickered to the console behind her, and Ariane moved. She darted at Hudson, whirling like a dancer in the ancient way her family's old Weapons Master had taught her as a girl. She might as well have attacked a plasteel bulkhead. Powerful arms caught and held her; the 'ruptor's muzzle came up against her head.

Shock held her utterly still for one blinding instant. Hudson's hand burned on her arm like the bitter cold of space.

"I don't have much to lose, Lady Ariane," Hudson said softly. "You'll call for clearance. Everything is perfectly—normal."

She considered fighting again; to put the *d'Artagnan* in a starjacker's hands was unthinkable.

But there was far more at stake. Marchand honor and Marchand interest demanded her safe return, to wed Wynn Slayton by inviolable contract that would bind their families forever. Her death now would gain nothing at all.

Clenching her teeth, Ariane hailed the prison port and made the final, in-person request for clearance. The bored officer's voice on the other end of the commlink never altered; her own was perfectly steady as she acknowledged her clearance to lift.

Abruptly Hudson let her go. "Very good," he murmured. "Take her up."

Ariane thought quickly as she dropped into the pilot's seat, Hudson breathing harshly over her shoulder. *He's only a boy. He can't know much about Caravel-class starships.* . . .

Her hand hovered just above the control stick. It shouldn't be too difficult to fool the young guard, make it seem as if they were leaving the system. And then—

Warm fingers feathered along her shoulder and slid under the thick hair at the base of her neck. "Oh no, Lady Ariane. It won't be so easy this time."

Her throat went dry as her hand fell from the console. Abruptly he let her go, stepping away. She turned in the seat to look up at the man who stood over her.

And he *changed*. As if he were made of something other than mere human flesh he began to change:

slowly, so slowly that at first she didn't realize what she was seeing.

The young man's softness vanished, cheekbones and hollows and sharp angles drawn forth from Hudson's unremarkable face. Sandy hair darkened in a slow wave under the uniform cap. An old scar snaked over skin tanned by relentless heat.

The eyes were the last to change. Blue faded, warmed, melted into copper.

Rook's eyes.

They held hers as he swept off his cap, freed the dark hair that fell to his shoulders.

The man who stood before her wore the tailored uniform of a Tantalan guard as a hellhound might wear a collar. A wild beast crouched on the deck of the *d'Artagnan*.

A Kalian.

Reaction coursed through her, numbing her hands and stopping her breath.

"*Mon Dieu*," she whispered. "You."

BEFORE I WAKE
by Terry Lawrence

Loveswept star Terry Lawrence is an extraordinary story-teller whose novels sizzle with irresistible wit and high-voltage passion. Now, she weaves the beloved fairy tale Sleeping Beauty into a story so enthralling it will keep you up long into the night. . . .

She came clean. "Gabe, I simply must apologize. I have something I'm sorry to tell you."

"You're married."

She croaked a laugh. "Ha ha. No." Her flippant wave fooled no one. She wasn't good with men. Actually, she wasn't bad. She'd had relationships. Some of them had proceeded all the way to bed and *then* they'd fallen apart. "We taped you."

"You what?"

She swung around in her chair and retrieved the black plastic box. When she swung back he was still smiling. This time a cautious glint lurked in his blue eyes.

"The night tech on duty in the sleep lab the evening you were here filmed you sleeping. It's common practice, we do it all the time."

"Do you?"

"I'm apologizing because we didn't have your permission."

"Ah." He took the tape from her, his tapering fingers touching hers. Their gazes met and held. "Did you watch it?"

Where were those stacks of folders when she needed a place to hide? "A little. You seemed to have slept well."

"Like the dead." One side of his mouth curved up.

She'd never noticed the way his brows arched, like Gothic windows in a gloomy cathedral. He had an air of the fallen angel about him, the devilish rogue, the lost soul. He'd referred to himself as something of the sort, though she couldn't remember exactly how.

She felt light-headed. The atmosphere was too close. She'd been lost in his eyes too long. She needed air. She could handle this. She rose, her legs shaking, and edged her way around her desk. From there to the window seemed like miles.

He turned his head, following her with his eyes. His body seemed unnaturally still. Hers seemed unbearably energized. Her pulse skittered through her veins. Her breath skimmed in and out of her lungs.

"So you've been sleeping better," she said, making conversation, gripping the window frame. The wood was ancient, the paint peeling and dry. She shoved. The frame didn't budge. Pressing her wrists against the chilly glass, she tried again. Her breath frosted the pane. She inhaled the musty odor of rotting wood.

Gabe reached around her from behind. She froze, her breath trapped in her lungs. He rested his thumbs on her knuckles, splaying his hands on either side of hers. In one sharp move he thrust the window upward. The wood screeched like an angry bird.

In the ensuing silence, traffic noise rose from the street below. Cold air flooded the room, slithering into the gaps of her coat, shocking her with its icy fingers. She turned with great effort. Sagging against the sill, she gripped the splintery wood on either side of her thighs.

Gabe rested his hands on her shoulders. "Shana."

His grogginess was long gone. A feral alertness sharpened his features. He lingered over her name like a starving man over a meal. His lids lowered. He concentrated on her lips. She longed to taste his.

She fought for air, for sense. She couldn't do this. Whirling in the tight circle of his arms, she flattened her palms against the glass. They instantly formed a misty outline, ten fingers clutching thin air.

His fingers closed over her wrists like talons capturing her hammering pulse. His thumbs curled into her damp palms. Mingled breaths frosted the pane, blotting out the world outside.

"Please," she panted. She was slipping, her will ebbing with every weak breath. This wasn't right. She pressed her cheek to the window, letting the mind-clearing reality of bitter cold bite into it. The chill penetrated her clothing, pebbling her breasts. The hard line of the sill pressed across her thighs.

An eerie incongruous warmth whispered across her face. His breath. He lifted her hair off her neck. She tried to protest. Her lips barely parted. "I can't believe we're doing this again."

"Believe."

"We can't."

"We can."

**And don't miss these spellbinding
romances from Bantam Books,
on sale in August:**

LORD OF THE DRAGON
by Suzanne Robinson

"An author with star quality . . . spectacularly
talented."
—*Romantic Times*

MARIANA
by Susanna Kearsley

Winner of the Catherine Cookson Prize for fiction

*To enter the sweepstakes outlined below, you must respond by the date specified and
follow all entry instructions published elsewhere in this offer.*

DREAM COME TRUE SWEEPSTAKES

Sweepstakes begins 9/1/94, ends 1/15/96. To qualify for the Early Bird Prize, entry must be received by the
date specified elsewhere in this offer. Winners will be selected in random drawings on 2/29/96 by an indepen-
ent judging organization whose decisions are final. Early Bird winner will be selected in a separate drawing
om among all qualifying entries.

Odds of winning determined by total number of entries received. Distribution not to exceed 300 million.

Estimated maximum retail value of prizes: Grand (1) $25,000 (cash alternative $20,000); First (1) $2,000;
cond (1) $750; Third (50) $75; Fourth (1,000) $50; Early Bird (1) $5,000. Total prize value: $86,500.

Automobile and travel trailer must be picked up at a local dealer; all other merchandise prizes will be
ipped to winners. Awarding of any prize to a minor will require written permission of parent/guardian. If a
ip prize is won by a minor, s/he must be accompanied by parent/legal guardian. Trip prizes subject to avail-
ility and must be completed within 12 months of date awarded. Blackout dates may apply. Early Bird trip is
a space available basis and does not include port charges, gratuities, optional shore excursions and onboard
rsonal purchases. Prizes are not transferable or redeemable for cash except as specified. No substitution for
izes except as necessary due to unavailability. Travel trailer and/or automobile license and registration fees
e winners' responsibility as are any other incidental expenses not specified herein.

Early Bird Prize may not be offered in some presentations of this sweepstakes. Grand through third prize
inners will have the option of selecting any prize offered at level won. All prizes will be awarded. Drawing will
held at 204 Center Square Road, Bridgeport, NJ 08014. Winners need not be present. For winners list (avail-
le in June, 1996), send a self-addressed, stamped envelope by 1/15/96 to: Dream Come True Winners, P.O.
ox 572, Gibbstown, NJ 08027.

THE FOLLOWING APPLIES TO THE SWEEPSTAKES ABOVE:

No purchase necessary. No photocopied or mechanically reproduced entries will be accepted. Not responsi-
e for lost, late, misdirected, damaged, incomplete, illegible, or postage-die mail. Entries become the property
sponsors and will not be returned.

Winner(s) will be notified by mail. Winner(s) may be required to sign and return an affidavit of eligibility/
lease within 14 days of date on notification or an alternate may be selected. Except where prohibited by law, entry
nstitutes permission to use of winners' names, hometowns, and likenesses for publicity without additional com-
nsation. Void where prohibited or restricted. All federal, state, provincial, and local laws and regulations apply.

All prize values are in U.S. currency. Presentation of prizes may vary; values at a given prize level will be
proximately the same. All taxes are winners' responsibility.

Canadian residents, in order to win, must first correctly answer a time-limited skill testing question admin-
ered by mail. Any litigation regarding the conduct and awarding of a prize in this publicity contest by a resi-
nt of the province of Quebec may be submitted to the Regie des loteries et courses du Quebec.

Sweepstakes is open to legal residents of the U.S., Canada, and Europe (in those areas where made avail-
le) who have received this offer.

Sweepstakes in sponsored by Ventura Associates, 1211 Avenue of the Americas, New York, NY 10036 and
esented by independent businesses. Employees of these, their advertising agencies and promotional compa-
es involved in this promotion, and their immediate families, agents, successors, and assignees shall be ineli-
ble to participate in the promotion and shall not be eligible for any prizes covered herein.   SWP 3/95

DON'T MISS THESE FABULOUS BANTAM WOMEN'S FICTION TITLES

On sale in July

DEFIANT
by PATRICIA POTTER
Winner of the 1992 *Romantic Times*
Career Achievement Award for Storyteller of the Year

Only the desire for vengeance had spurred Wade Foster on, until the last of the men who had destroyed his family lay sprawled in the dirt. Now, badly wounded, the rugged outlaw closed his eyes against the pain . . . and awoke to the tender touch of the one woman who could show him how to live—and love—again.
_____ 56601-6 $5.50/$6.99

STAR-CROSSED
by nationally bestselling author SUSAN KRINARD

"Susan Krinard was born to write romance."
—New York Times *bestselling author Amanda Quick*

A captivating futuristic romance in the tradition of Johanna Lindsey, Janelle Taylor, and Kathleen Morgan. A beautiful aristocrat risks a forbidden love . . . with a dangerously seductive man born of an alien race.
_____ 56917-1 $4.99/$5.99

BEFORE I WAKE
by TERRY LAWRENCE

"Terry Lawrence is a magnificent writer." —Romantic Times

Award-winning author Terry Lawrence is an extraordinary storyteller whose novels sizzle with irresistible wit and high-voltage passion. Now, she weaves the beloved fairy tale *Sleeping Beauty* into a story so enthralling it will keep you up long into the night.
_____ 56914-7 $5.50/$6.99